Run from the King

Emma Brant

Copyright © 2024 by [Author or Pen Name]

All rights reserved.

No portion of this book may be reproduced in any form without written permission from the publisher or author, except as permitted by U.S. copyright law.

Contents

1. Prologue — 1
2. Chapter 1 — 10
3. Chapter 2 — 17
4. Chapter 3 — 27
5. Chapter 4 — 35
6. Chapter 5 — 42
7. Chapter 6 — 51
8. Chapter 7 — 60
9. Chapter 8 — 67
10. Chapter 9 — 78
11. Chapter 10 — 88
12. Chapter 11 — 98
13. Chapter 12 — 109
14. Chapter 13 — 122
15. Chapter 14 — 130

16. Chapter 15 — 139
17. Chapter 16 — 146
18. Chapter 17 — 157
19. Chapter 18 — 168
20. Chapter 19 — 178
21. Chapter 20 — 186
22. Chapter 21 — 193
23. Chapter 22 — 201
24. Chapter 23 — 207
25. Epilogue — 218

Prologue

"Honey, dinner will be ready soon. Can you go get the kids?" Brittany asked Erik while he was working in the forge.

"Yes, dear. I'll go get them in a minute." Erik replied, pausing to wipe sweat from his brow. Working in the forge all day has kept him in peak physical shape, however, the heat alone would make any man sweat. Slaving away, Erik continued hitting hammer on metal, muscles tensing with each hit, hammering the item into the shape he desired.

Erik not only made tools, he also made weapons to trade in town. A town that lay a few days away. Weapons of his quality always sold high compared to the cost he got his materials, that was the price for a blacksmith of his skill. People from all over the country would come to get a weapon made by him, his skills were highly sought of. After the third war, though, Erik took his love and left the world behind them.

They didn't want any more to do with a world at war with itself, instead, the two of them wanted to live in the wild, living off the land. It was only after their first child that Erik decided to pick up blacksmithing again to help keep food on the table.

"Honey!" Brittany yelled, standing in the doorway tapping her foot impatiently.

"Sorry my love! I lost track of time!" Erik replied, dropping his work on the bench. "I'll go get them now, we will be back before you know it!" He continued, kissing his wife on the cheek as he hurried out the door, towards the woods where he knew their children liked to play.

"Rina! Don't run so far ahead!" Aiden yelled, running after his younger sister. "You'll get lost!" Ellie barked in agreement, as she too chased after Rina. Rina was a stubborn child, always wanting to explore the unknown, which usually got her into trouble in some form or another. "Rina?" Aiden called out when he could no longer see her.

"Rina!?" He yelled again, his eyes darting left to right, sweat starting to drip from his forehead as he searched for her. "Rina! Where are you!?"

"Boo!" She yelled, jumping out from behind a tree, causing Aiden to flinch and Ellie to bark excitedly, wagging her tail as she ran around Rina. "Hi Ellie! Did you miss me?"

"That's not funny!" Aiden sighed. "Mom would have killed me if anything happened to you!" he continued, lightly punching his sister in the arm. "Where have you gotten us lost now?" He asked, looking at their surroundings, unsure of where they were.

"Hmm." Rina replied, looking around as well. "I... Think... We're in the woods still!" She mocked, laughing at her brother, seeing that he was getting frustrated at being lost. Aiden hated being lost, he was smart and liked things to be in order, Rina being the complete opposite. Which caused Aiden a lot of stress when it was just the two of them playing.

She loved to run off and explore the woods, not caring which direction she went or what waited for them. Aiden always wanted to leave some sort of markings on trees that he could use to find his way back, he had a little book that he would draw his own map of the woods. Aiden loved to explore as much as his sister did, he only wanted to keep a record of their journeys and anything they found.

"Ha... Ha..." Aiden retorted. "Seriously though, where are we? I don't recognize this area, and these trees don't look anything like the ones that we've seen."

Looking around, Rina started to realize just how far she had ran. Even though she was adventurous, she was still only eight years old and frightened easily. "Aiden... I don't like it here anymore. I want to go home!" She whined, looking up as the first drops of rain dripped on her face.

"Of course, you do." Aiden sighed. "Ellie, take us home girl!" he told their dog, hoping that she would know what he meant. "Home? You know, where the food is." At the word food, he got a bark from Ellie and her bouncing around in excitement. "Of course, you would know what food means." Aiden smiled, petting Ellie on the head.

The three of them turned around, heading back in the direction that they came from. Aiden tried to find something that looked familiar, or a clearing so he could see where the sun was positioned, however, the trees were too thick for them to see the sky and it was only getting darker.

The rain started to fall harder, dripping its way through the trees above. They heard sounds of insects and birds all around them, the latter giving the forest an eerie feel. Aiden pulled out his book, looking over his notes and maps he had created of the area surrounding their home. He had different kinds of trees, animals, and any unique areas marked in his notes, anything he could use as landmarks. "I don't see anything I recognize."

Ellie yipped quietly as she sniffed, her hair standing on edge. "Stand behind me Rina, everything will be ok." Aiden told his sister, pulling out a dagger that his father had made him. "We will keep you safe." Ellie barked, agreeing that she, too, will keep Rina safe.

The three of them heard rustling coming from the bushes behind them, causing all three to jump, changing directions to face the source of the noise. The rustling came from a few yards away and only got louder as the source moved closer to them. As suddenly as the rustling appeared, all went quiet for a few minutes, making them uneasy.

The sounds of the birds and insects seemed to have vanished, the only sound they heard was that of the rain falling through the trees, dripping on them from above. Backs against the trunk of a cold, rigid tree, they waited and waited, not wanting to get caught off guard by whatever lay in the bushes, watching them from afar. Aiden was positive it was some sort of creature that wanted them for a snack.

Again, came a rustling noise from the bushes, this time closer, leaves swooshing as whatever came for them inched its way towards the trio, snorting quietly as it moved. Aiden signaled for Rina and Ellie to be quiet, raising one finger to his mouth. He tried to mentally prepare himself for anything as he gripped his dagger tightly, hands shaking from fear and the cold water that dripped from the trees, soaking him.

This time, the rustling noise came from the bush right in front of them, there was no mistaking it, the beast wanted them, and it knew where they were. The three waited for the creature to make the first move, scared to move in any direction, fearing that it would catch them from behind.

Seconds later, what felt like an eternity to Aiden, a large boar, twice the size of him, came barreling out of the bushes, charging straight for them. Aiden was the first to react, pushing Rina aside, and dodging the boar at the last moment as it ran past him.

Ellie was the next, with faster reflexes, she had dodged the boar and leapt on its back, biting down on it furiously, trying to protect her family. Rina was still on the ground, when Aiden got to his feet, running towards the boar to attack it with Ellie. Where Ellie went for the back, causing the creature to flail around, trying to get her off, Aiden moved around, looking for the chance to attack its legs.

When the boar moved left, Aiden would go right, trying to get in its blind spot. (Never fight a larger opponent head on, use your wit, go for their legs, slowing them so you can out maneuver them, be cautious though, even a wounded enemy can land a lucky strike that can finish their opponent.) His father's voice echoed in his head.

The boar was unpredictable with Ellie on its back, changing its directions constantly. Aiden would attempt to move closer only to back away seconds before being trampled as the beast turned frantically. "There!" Aiden said to himself, lunging forward, sliding by the creature's hind legs, slicing just behind the knee, the blade slashing deep into the skin.

Rain poured down through the trees, dousing the trio as they fought desperately. Wiping water out of his eyes, Aiden stood ready, waiting for his next opportunity to strike. The boar still fought as if nothing happened, trying as hard as it could, all of its focus on trying to free its back from Ellies vicious attacks. Rina sat where Aiden pushed her, watching in horror, trembling as Aiden went for the beast again, sliding for the legs, dagger in hand.

The boar's movement caused Aiden's attack to go from a slice to a stab, lodging the blade in the boar's leg. Enraged, the hog turned, too quickly for Aiden to react, headbutting him in the chest, sending him and his dagger flying into a nearby tree. Rina screamed, terrified, as she saw her brother slam into the trunk. She rushed to his side, tears streaming down her face. "Are... are you okay Aiden?" She asked, as she checked him for any wounds.

"I'm alright..." He grunted, trying to get to his feet, only to fail. "We have to help Ellie. She's not going to be able to stop it on her own." He continued realizing Ellie was no longer on its back. She had left bite and claw marks all over the hairy back of the boar and was now running circles around it.

Thanks to Aiden's last attack, the creature was weakened and could not maneuver as fast as before. Aiden knew, though, it would only take one good hit from that boar to stop Ellie. Although she was an agile and strong dog, she was not a large one, weighing only about forty pounds. "We have to help..." Aiden stated, trying to stand up again, and falling back to his knees, his injury being worse than he thought.

Rain dripped from above, hums of birds chirping echoed the forest, sounds of insects berated them in full force. Shaking her head, Rina glanced down, seeing her reflection in the blade of the dagger. Dread filling her heart, she wanted to protect her brother, knowing that it was all her fault for getting them lost. Thunder cracked in the sky, causing Rina to flinch as she stared at her image in the blade.

Tears flowing down her cheeks, with watery determination in her eyes, Rina picked up the weapon, shakily holding it in both hands. "I will protect you Aiden."

The two looked up as they heard Ellie yelp. "Where is she?" Rina asked, her eyes darting back and forth, searching for any signs of Ellie. Rain continued to pour down through the trees, drenching everything around them. Rina saw only the angry boar, blood and water dripping from its back as it kicked up mud, preparing to charge them.

"Don't take your eyes off the boar!" Aiden told Rina, as he slowly got to his feet, using the tree for support. "Back away slowly and get away from here!" He yelled, grabbing the dagger from her and pushing her behind him. Aiden shoved himself away from the tree, stumbling in the direction of the beast, taunting it, flailing his arms up in the air, trying his best to get its attention so Rina could escape.

The boar snorted, causing snot and blood to shoot from its nostrils. With its wounded legs, it began to awkwardly charge him, stumbling as it ran towards Aiden. Try as he could, Aiden was too weak to dodge the creature. The boar was seconds away from trampling him.

"Nooooooo!" Rina yelled, watching as the boar closed the gap between it and her brother. The creature was only a few feet away from trampling Aiden, its massive body running the best it could, suffering from the wounds in its legs and all the bites that Ellie had given it.

Aiden closed his eyes, bracing for the boar's assault, an assault that didn't seem to come. Opening one of his eyes, he saw the boar flailing around as its face was on fire. No longer did the creature seek Aiden and Rina, it's only concern was to put out the fire. He watched, in shock, the boar roar in pain as it ran off, back into the woods, face full of flames. Aiden looked back at his younger sister, who stood there stunned, staring at her hands, unsure what she had done.

"Rina!" Aiden yelled, snapping her back from her daze. "We have to find Ellie and get home!" Nodding, Rina helped Aiden search the bushes nearby, only taking them a couple of minutes to find Ellie laying in the shrubs. "Are you ok Ellie?" Aiden asked, kneeling to check her for wounds. "She's alright Rina, she just got knocked around like I did." He laughed, coughing in pain. "You're going to have to help her get back, I will be fine." She nodded without a word, tears still running down her face.

Aiden looked up, seeing rays of sunshine breaking through the trees as the last drops of rain fell on his face. Wiping the sweat and grime from his forehead, he still couldn't believe what had happened. Aiden tried his best to process the situation, trying to come up with any answer other than his little sister had used magic.

"Aiden! Rina! Where are you!?" A voice came in the distance, catching their attention.

"Daddy! We're over here!" Rina yelled back, snapping out of her distraught at the sound of her father. Soon as he was in sight, she ran into his arms, crying. "It's all my fault daddy!"

"It's ok baby." Erik replied, picking her up in his arms and walked towards Aiden and Ellie. "Are you ok Aiden? How's Ellie?"

"We're okay Dad. A boar attacked us, Ellie managed to scare it off, but got hit when it ran away." Aiden replied, looking at Rina's confused expression. She knew that he would tell her why he lied later. "I'll be fine, but can you help Ellie Dad?"

"Of course." Erik replied, giving his son a hug. "I'm proud of you, you protected your sister." He continued, as he picked up Ellie, holding her in his arms, who now was wide awake, licking him all over his face. "Yes, I'm proud of you too Ellie." He laughed. "Let's go home."

Chapter 1

"What happened?!" Brittany yelled while checking Aiden for wounds, lifting his shirt to see bruising across his ribs and back.

"I'm sorry mommy! It's my fault..." Rina replied, tears rolling down her face. "I ran off and didn't watch where I was going, we got lost..." She continued, looking at the floor in front of her, not daring to meet her mother's gaze, fiddling her hands behind her back. "I'm really sorry mommy."

Seeing that Aiden was ok, except minor bruising, Brittany sighed and picked Rina up. "It's ok baby girl, you have to be careful and not go so far into the woods where you get lost. You're lucky you had Aiden and Ellie there." Brittany continued, hugging her daughter tightly. "Promise me that you'll be more careful."

"I promise mommy!" Rina said, hugging her mother tight, her little arms reaching around her. "You should have seen the way Aiden and Ellie fought off the boar! They were awesome!" she said enthusiastically, throwing her hands in the air and making a face as if she was eating. "Ellie was on its back biting it for so long, and

Aiden attacked its legs. I can't believe how good they were! I want to be like them!"

"In time Rina." Erik said, patting Aiden on the back. "He has trained a lot to be as good as he is. If that's what you want, then you need to put in that training too. However, I think that you'll do better like your mother, with a bow and arrow. You know that's more fun and less scary, right?" He said, poking Rina in her belly, tickling her.

"I'm not scared anymore daddy!" Rina replied defiantly, pushing his hand away.

"She held her own too, dad. When I could barely stand, she took my dagger and stood in front of me, determined to keep me safe." Aiden said, smiling at his younger sister.

"Maybe we should teach her both ways, honey." Brittany offered. "Would you like that Rina?"

"Yes! Yes! Yes!" Rina replied, beaming with joy. "Can we start now? Please!"

"No sweetie, it's dinner, then you two need to get some rest. You both had a long day." Brittany answered, kissing Rina on the cheek as she put her down.

"Aww, okay mommy."

They all sat down for dinner together, reliving their tale of the giant boar attack. Rina bounced with excitement whenever it came to her learning how to fight like Aiden. She imagined having a weapon just like he did, imitating slicing and stabbing an imaginary enemy over the dinner table.

It took all her willpower to keep quiet about the fire. She had yet to talk with Aiden about it, but he wanted to keep that from them. With the way he threw himself at the boar to protect her, she trusted his judgment. She had no idea how it happened but knew that she was the source of the fire.

She wanted to protect her brother from being hurt, she wished for the power to protect him, and somehow her wish was granted. After a while, their parents began talking about stuff that she lost interest in, they usually talked about the tools that her father made, or when the next time he was heading into town. All Rina could think of is how she summoned the fire, she knew that she did it, she felt it within her soul.

After dinner, Erik got the bath ready for Aiden. He got the water from the well behind the house, and lit the furnace below the tub, heating the water for Aiden to soak his wounds. "Thanks dad. I'll be okay." Aiden said, as he shut the door to the bathroom. Aiden winced from the pain as he eased himself into the tub, feeling the bruised ribs that he got thanks to the boar. He slid down, leaving only his face, from the nose up, above the water, staring at the ceiling. Aiden was lost in thought about how they were almost killed, despite how his parents played it off, he knew they almost died.

Yet, against all odds, they lived. Rina somehow managed to use magic. He was unsure how to react about the situation. He did not know much about magic, only what his father had told him. That magic was a very rare trait, and a dangerous one to have. That there were two types of magic users, Wizards and Sorcerers. Sorcerers were Wizards, at some point in their life, who made sacrifices to gain power beyond that of a Wizard. He had said that not all magic users are bad, not all were good, and most probably don't know they have the abilities.

"Mommy, what's it like to fight?" Rina asked Brittany, resting her chin on the table. She stared at her mother while she was washing the dishes, remembering the stories Brittany told her when she was younger.

"Well dear, it's not something that I want you to experience, but it's something I want you to be prepared for." Brittany replied, placing the last dish on the counter. "It's very stressful and scary. You will never know when you may take your last breath. In the war, there were many times I thought I was going to die, but then your father managed to save me or give me the strength to fight on."

"When you have someone you care deeply for, it doesn't matter how bad your body aches, how tired you feel, the energy that you need to survive will be there.

That is what you experienced today with your brother. Both you and Aiden found that energy to fight for each other." Brittany continued, sitting next to her daughter. Rina absorbed every word her mother told her. "I need you to promise me that everything we teach you, that you will take it seriously and be very careful. This is not a game to be played or skills to use on anyone for amusement. We are going to teach you how to defend yourself and protect your loved ones, because some day, you may need to."

"I promise mommy!" Rina replied, giving her mother a giant hug.

"You're growing up so fast!" Brittany commented, hugging Rina tightly. "I think I hear Aiden getting out of the bath, go wash up and get ready for bed. You had a long day and need your rest."

"Why did you not tell daddy about the fire?" Rina questioned Aiden as she sat down on the floor next to him.

"Shh..." Aiden replied, getting up to close the door. "It's because what dad told me about magic."

Aiden began pacing the room, thinking of the best way to explain to his sister that she can do something that is dangerous, yet something he wished he was able to do.

(Magic is used by two types of people, Wizards and Sorcerers. Wizards vary in skill from novice to masters. They were used a lot in the first and second war. Only to diminish in numbers. Now, there's none that anyone knows about. Sorcerer's, on the other hand, are masters at their craft. They were once Wizards who made a great sacrifice to gain unimaginable power. These magic users are not the friendliest of people. Again, there are not many, I only know of one. King of Kaskia, Cladon. In the third war, he was searching for anyone with magical abilities. I don't know why, but I pity anyone he found that could use magic.) His father's voice echoed in his head.

"What is it?" Rina asked, worried at the troubled look on Aiden's face.

"You just have to be careful. It's dangerous and a skill that bad people are after. I think dad would get worried if he found out what you did." Aiden replied, plopping down on the floor. "He seems to have a lot on his mind already with the winter coming in a few months."

"I want to learn how to control it, I don't want to hurt anyone on accident." Rina stated with a tear strolling down her cheek. "I want to be able to protect my family the way you protected me!"

Hugging his sister, Aiden replied. "I will help as much as I can."

"Do you know how long you will be gone honey?" Brittany asked, as she finished cleaning up the table.

"Two days, maybe three. It depends on the weather and how the roads are. Last time the roads were too muddy, the horses couldn't pull the cart until it dried out." Erik responded, giving Brittany a hand with the trash.

"I worry every time you have to leave." Brittany stated, stopping to hold her husband. "You know they're still looking for you, for us."

"I know, my love. But we need supplies before the winter, the more we push it off, the smaller the chance of making it to Osion in time to get what we need." Erik said, giving his wife a kiss on her forehead. "Besides, Ellie will be with me." Ellie barked as she heard the mention of her name. "See? She agrees that everything will be fine."

"Where am I?" Rina thought to herself, looking around a room that was not hers. She ran towards the window when she heard screams coming from outside. Placing her hand against the glass, she saw people running through the cobblestone streets, being chased by four armed soldiers. She clenched her fist, slamming it against the window as she watched the soldiers catch up to and kill the people who were running. Rina turned to look in the other direction.

She heard someone shout, but was unable to make out what the man said. She saw a single man stand behind the soldiers, sword in his hand, challenging them. The soldiers laughed at the man, walking towards him confidently. With speed she had never seen before, Rina saw the man charge the soldiers, too fast for them to react. By the time the soldiers realized it, the first one was dead, the second having a blade sticking into his chest. The last two tried to attack the man, only to be killed themselves seconds later.

The streets became dark, dust and smoke filling the air. The man vanished from her sight, as the sounds of the war outside faded. Rina turned towards the dresser, walking to it slowly. The room became hazy, she watched as her hand reached for the top drawer, a hand that was not her own.

Fingers wrapping around the handle, pulling the drawer open, revealing a sword that glimmered through the haze. The hand picked up the sword, lifting it towards her face, examining the blade. Rina saw the eyes in the reflection, eyes that were not her own, eyes of an older woman. The woman raised an eyebrow as she looked into Rina's eyes, locking their eyes together in the reflection. Rina felt all her power draining from her, her eyelids getting heavy, sweat forming on her forehead. She felt as if she was being put under some sort of spell, a spell she fought with all her might, trying to open her eyes.

Rina sprung from her bed, sitting straight up, covered in sweat. Glancing down at her hands, she turned them over multiple times, making sure that they were hers. She looked around, seeing that she was back in her own bedroom. "It was only a dream." She sighed.

Chapter 2

"Aiden! Grab those tools and put them in the sack too." Erik told his son, pointing at a pile of tools, ranging from hammers, sheers, kitchen pots and pans. "Then put the sack in the back of the cart."

"Yes dad." Aiden replied, sulking as he grabbed each item, dropping them into the sack. "Why can't I go with you?"

"You know that you're not old enough for that yet." Erik answered, dismissing any further arguments about the subject. "Where did I put it?" He muttered, looking through his workshop, moving random objects aside that he had been working on, only to leave it unfinished to start a new project. "There it is!"

Aiden watched as his father pulled a sword from under a pile of scrap metal. Wondering why his father would need to take the weapon with him on a trip to the village just to sell supplies. Seeing the look on his son's face, Erik commented. "It's for safety. You never know if a wild animal, or worse, bandits may attack. Better to have it and not need it than to not have it and need it."

With the cart loaded, Erik said his goodbyes to his family. Hopping on the front seat of the wagon, he whistled for Ellie to join him. Eagerly, she jumped up onto the seat next to him, tail wagging happily. With a whip of the reins, Erik and Ellie trotted down the road, fading into the trees.

"Mom? Can Rina and I go play by the lake for a bit?" Aiden asked, hoping that the two of them would have some time alone to see what Rina was able to do. Aiden was anxious to find out if she truly was capable of using magic.

"Yes dear." Brittany answered. "But be back for lunch. After that we will go back to the lake and go fishing for dinner."

Aiden and Rina excitedly ran into the woods, knowing the way to the lake they had visited many times growing up. The two raced each other, dodging trees, bushes, and the occasional squirrel that bolted from their hiding places. Only taking a few minutes to get there, the duo burst from the woods to see a beautiful lake resting in the middle of the forest. Aiden walked towards the dock that his father had built when he was only a couple of years old and stared across the water. Rina strolled up beside him, staring at her brother. "What are you thinking?"

"Just thinking about how big the world is and if I will ever get to explore it." Aiden gestured to the other side of the lake. "I know we're not supposed to go to the other side, but I'm curious what's over there and beyond these woods."

"You will get to see it all one day!" Rina replied, encouraging her brother that he could see the world.

"Right." Aiden exhaled. "Magic time! Do you remember how you felt when you did it yesterday?"

"Umm. I was scared you were going to get hurt." Rina answered, rubbing tears from her eyes at the memory.

"Good. Use that feeling." Aiden replied, walking the shore of the lake. "No. Not this one." He muttered, picking up a small rock and dropping it back down. "This one, and that one." He continued as he gathered a few rocks together, placing them into a small circle near the water's edge.

"What are you doing?" Rina questioned.

"Stay here, I'll be right back. I need a stick." Aiden stated, running towards the woods briefly, then coming back with a giant stick in his hand. "This, this is your target." He continued, breaking the stick over his knee, into four even parts. Stabbing the first one into the ground at the center of the rocks. Confused, Rina nodded. Moving where her brother told her to stand, waiting as he prepared what he was doing.

"There!" Aiden said triumphantly. "That feeling, focus on it. Imagine that little stick is the boar and do what you did yesterday."

"Okay." Rina answered, concentrating on the attack from the day before. Her eyes watering as she remembered the thought of her brother being hit into a tree. "I don't feel the same thing." She stated, looking down at her hand.

"Hmm." Aiden muttered, thinking of another way to help his sister to manifest her magic. "Maybe try thinking of fire too?"

Standing there, determined to set the stick on fire, Rina wiped the tears from her eyes as the look on her face changed into stone cold determination. Raising her hand, body trembling, Rina tried with all her might to summon fire on the stick, sweat dripping from her brow, her knees quivering from exhaustion, a small spark burst into existence then faded away from where it came. Collapsing to the ground, Rina fought to catch her breath.

"Are you ok?" Aiden asked, rushing to her side. "I'm sorry Rina, we shouldn't do this, it's too much."

"No!" Rina rebelled, to herself as much as to her brother. "I can do this!"

"Take a breather for now. Catch your breath." Aiden said, pulling a container from his belt that held water. "Drink."

Doing as he said, Rina grabbed the flask of water, drank, and relaxed. "Did you see it?"

"See what?" Aiden said, shrugging his shoulders.

"A spark!" Rina said, excitedly once her energy began to come back. "I got a spark!"

"You did?!" Aiden asked, looking back at the stick, seeing a small burn mark on one of the rocks. "You did!"

Rina attempted to summon fire again. On and on throughout the morning, she would try, fail, fall to her knees, then get back up and try again. Try as she could, she was only able to manage small sparks, all missing her target. She left most of the rocks with burn marks, and once caught the grass on fire from a spark that landed past her target. Aiden managed to stomp the fire out before it had spread. Neither the fire she almost started, nor exhaustion deterred her.

Before they knew it, the sun was well above their heads. "We need to head home for lunch." Aiden stated. "You need rest too."

Reluctant to stop, Rina nodded, too tired to argue. Where they ran to the lake before, the two walked home in silence. Aiden was stunned at the progress his sister was making in such a short time. Rina's mind was racing with thoughts as to how she can make it work, ways to pull the energy she needed. She thought of why she kept missing her target, analyzing how she felt when the spark completely missed the circle of rocks. She processed each attempt and failure to light the stick, thinking of any way of improving.

"You two are late!" Brittany scolded. "Hurry up before your food gets colder."

Brittany and her children ate quietly, all having too many thoughts on their minds. Brittany worried about her husband, who has been gone for half a day already. She worried that he will run into trouble because of their past. Aiden wondered what Rina was capable of, remembering his talks with his father about Wizards and Sorcerers and the power they wield.

Rina could not stop thinking of ways to recreate the magic she had used against the boar, she thought maybe if she changed the way she stood, the way she thought, or if there was something else that would help her summon the power she had the day before.

"Come on kids. Go get your fishing poles." Brittany said, breaking the silence.

Without a word, both Aiden and Rina put their dishes away and walked outside. "I don't want to fish Aiden." Rina pouted, walking to the shed where their rods lay.

"I know." Aiden replied, knowing that she wants to practice more. "If we don't have time today, we will try some more tomorrow, okay?"

"Okay." Rina Frowned.

"Are you ready?" Brittany asked as she, too, grabbed her fishing pole.

"Yes mom." Both kids answered in unison.

Brittany, Rina, and Aiden walked quietly through the woods until Aiden broke the silence. "You were in the war with dad, right mom?"

"Yes, dear." Brittany answered. "Why do you ask?"

"I'm just curious about it. The people you fought with and against." Aiden replied, ducking under a tree branch.

"Well. The simple answer: we fought against Premus. The neighboring country." Brittany replied. "Once, Kaskia was a part of Premus. There was a rebellion that won its freedom, then they formed Kaskia."

"As for who we fought with." Brittany continued. "It was a varying army. People of different ancestries, and creatures created by Cladon."

"Who's that mommy?" Rina asked, never having heard the name before.

"He's the King of Kaskia, supposedly he's been King for three-hundred years since the forming of Kaskia." Brittany answered. "Find your spot you want to fish from." She continued, pointing at the dock. "I'll continue the story when we start fishing."

Aiden and Rina eagerly found their spots on the dock, wanting to hear more about the history of the country they lived in, a country that they knew very little of outside the woods.

"From what I remember, we fought alongside the Felien and the Kaiine, I think even a Bermion or two were in the ranks." Brittany said, as if that information alone would have been enough for her children.

"Fe...line? Kainie? Bermion?" Rina questioned, having trouble pronouncing the names.

"Fe-lien, Kai-ine." Brittany corrected. "Felien were supposedly created by Cladon in the first war. They remind me of giant cats that walk on two legs. They're furry and range in color too. Kaiine are their counterparts, they're like Ellie but stand upright and are fierce fighters. I believe they came from across the mountains, I don't think there's too many in Kaskia anymore."

"Bermion, well, they're bears." Brittany stated. "I know you've seen bears in the wild when we go hunting, but those are not the same as Bermion. Bermion are highly intelligent beings. I've only met a few and know about a few more than that. Not much is known about them or where they come from."

Aiden and Rina listened quietly as their mother told them stories of the war. Fights where they were sure to have been defeated, but her and their father managed to fight their way out, enemy after enemy they defeated everyone that stood in their way. They listened as she told them stories of great battles between Kaskia and Premus, and then the stealth missions that lead them to the capital of Premus.

Before they knew it, the sun was already low on the horizon. Picking up the basket with the few fish they had caught, Brittany and her two children walked home. Both Aiden and Rina would question parts of her stories, asking for more details or clarification on what happened. "Go clean up for dinner. I will have it ready in a few minutes." Brittany told them soon as they walked into their home.

"Mommy, can you tell us about magic?" Rina asked, as she sat down at the table. Seeing Aiden glare at her for the question.

"Sure sweetie." Brittany answered. "There's two types of people that use magic. Wizards and Sorcerers. Wizards use all sorts of magic, elemental, summoning, healing, nature, and other types I do not know about. There's only a few Wizards in Kaskia and Premus that I know of. One is actually a Bermion, he's supposedly very old and very wise."

"Sorcerers, though, focus more on dark magic." She continued. "They use their magic to get more powerful. Cladon, he is the only Sorcerer that I know of. I hope that there will never be any more, but sadly, I know another will appear someday. Why are you two so curious today?"

"It was the boar." Aiden answered before Rina could utter a word. "It got us thinking of battles and what to expect in the future."

"Always thinking ahead, aren't you Aiden?" Brittany laughed. "Is there anything else you would like to know?"

"Why does dad have so many weapons?" Aiden asked flatly between bites of his meal.

"Well." Brittany coughed. "As you know, he is very skilled in making tools. During the war, he made many weapons and was a fierce fighter. He can use pretty much any weapon you can think of. He is truly a master of his craft."

"During the war, his crafting skills were highly sought. He even got noticed by Cladon, the King himself. Erik made weapons for the army towards the end of the war and continued to make them after. The king demanded it." Brittany sighed. "And you don't go against the King."

"He was bound to the King. He even had his own forge in the Capital. It was not the life he wanted, the life we wanted." She continued, her gaze drifting off into the distance. "We were madly in love and didn't want the war life anymore. We wanted to start a family."

"So, one night. We snuck out of the Capital and ran. We made ourselves disappear. We tried living in villages, he would make tools for trade, I would hunt for food. But Kaskian Soldiers were always on our heels. Once I became pregnant with you Aiden." She continued, placing her hand on his. "We decided to truly disappear. That's when we headed into the woods and built this home for ourselves." She added, gesturing to the house around them. "We only leave if we need supplies for the winter."

"Is that why you get worried every time he leaves?" Aiden asked.

"Yes, dear." Brittany answered, holding her necklace in her hands. "That's why he has the weapons. In case they find us. He will defend all of us." She continued, as a tear rolled down her cheek. "No more questions. It's late and you two need to get to bed."

Rina ran down the cobblestone street, looking behind her sporadically, checking for her pursuers. She didn't know why she was running, she just knew she had to keep moving. If she stopped, they would find her. The sounds of battle echoed across the city as the sun descended on the horizon.

Any time she heard sounds of swords clashing getting too close, Rina would duck between buildings, using the shadows to escape unnoticed. Rina stopped in her tracks when she turned a corner and ran into three soldiers. Soldiers who raised their weapons and charged at her. Rina froze, dread filling her body.

The soldiers would be upon her any second, yet she couldn't run. She tried to scream in terror, only to be muffled, her voice had abandoned her. The first soldier was upon her, she knew this would be it, the end, she wished she could be back home, back where it was safe. The soldier's attack was blocked by a sword, a sword that was being held by a hand that was hers but not. The sword was raised above her, holding the soldier back. Rina looked into the blade, seeing those eyes, the eyes that stared back at her.

Rina opened her eyes and headed to the mirror on her wall to see her reflection staring back at her. Shaking her head clear of the dream, she walked back to her bed and laid down. "No more please." She said as she pulled the blankets over her head, trying to hide from her dreams that were becoming nightmares.

Chapter 3

"Hurry up Aiden!" Rina yelled, anxious to get back to practicing her magic.

"Hold on! I'm looking for my dagger!" Aiden yelled back from his room. He rummaged through his dresser and pile of clothes laying at the foot of his bed. "Got it!" He shouted triumphantly, holding his dagger up. He quickly put the dagger in its sheath resting on his belt and ran out of the house to join his sister.

Rina waited by the nearest tree to the woods, taping her foot impatiently. "About time!" She chided. "I have a couple of ideas that I want to try!"

"What ideas?" Aiden questioned, his eyebrow arching out of curiosity.

"You'll have to wait and see." Rina replied, smiling as she skipped into the forest. "Do you think it's going to rain again?"

"No." Aiden answered, looking at the clouds in the sky. "They're not dark enough."

Aiden questioned and pried, trying to get her to tell him her ideas. He wanted to know what she came up with to help her accomplish her goal. He was so focused on getting the information out of her, Aiden did not see the low branch, and walked right into it, knocking him to the ground. Rina burst out laughing so hard that she tripped over a root and fell to the ground next to her brother.

Both Aiden and Rina sat in the grass, laughing so hard tears started forming in their eyes. After a few minutes of amusement, the pair got back to their feet and continued heading towards the lake, Aiden choosing to focus on his path over questioning his sister.

"Okay. Don't watch. Go train or something while I practice." Rina told her brother as they entered the clearing where the lake waited for them. Rina ran off before he could question her more, not wanting him watching as she tested her ideas.

"Okay, fine. I'll be right over there. Be careful please. Mom will shoot me if anything happens to you!" Aiden yelled, as she ran towards the stick and pile of rocks they made for target practice.

Rina watched Aiden as he pulled out his dagger, flipping it between both hands before stabbing and slicing an imaginary foe. She watched him cut an opponent in front of him, slide the dagger in the opposite direction, then stab the next enemy behind him. Without losing a step, he tossed the dagger from his dominant hand to the other, swinging it around in a fluid motion to take out the last attacker.

Determined to be as good as Aiden was, she focused hard on her magic. She knew she could summon fire, it was just a matter of unlocking the technique of how. Rina sat down, crossed her legs, and faced the circle of rocks with the stick protruding from the ground. She closed her eyes and thought about the boar, the sweat and grime that dripped from it, the snarl that sent snot flying from its nostrils, the stench of the beast.

She focused so hard that she could sense the beast as if it was in front of her. She focused harder, pinning her attention on the creature's face, then she changed the image of the face in her head to that of the stick. She knew it rested in the ground in front of her, a target that was not moving. "I can do this..." She muttered to herself. Rina felt the sweat dripping down her face. "I can do this..." She muttered again.

"Rina!" Aiden yelled.

Snapping her eyes open, her focus shattered, Rina looked at Aiden confused. "What?"

"Look..." Aiden said, his jaw dropped as he pointed in the direction of the stick.

Glancing where he pointed, Rina gasped. "I... I did that?" She stuttered in awe, staring at a hole in the ground that was charred and black. "What happened?!" She asked, turning to face Aiden, scared of what she had done.

"I was watching you for like twenty minutes. You were so focused. .." Aiden said. "You were muttering to yourself and next thing I know a fireball blew up the stick and that spot was on fire! Full on fire!"

"I... I... I didn't even notice... I thought I just started." Rina replied, shaking at the power of the fire she had summoned. "I don't want to do this anymore!" She said, crying that she could have hurt him and not noticed.

"It's okay Rina." Aiden consoled, hugging his sister. "You were amazing! You had the fire contained, I was worried for you. If that was a normal fire, it would have spread, but it didn't. It stayed within the circle of rocks. How did you even do that?"

"I just... I focused on the boar, what it looked like, smelled like, and then I switched to the stick." Rina answered, wiping tears from her eyes. "I'm scared Aiden..."

"It's okay Rina, we'll stop for now. Would you like to go exploring?" Aiden asked, pulling his sister to her feet.

"Okay." Rina muttered, looking down at the hole that she left in the ground.

Aiden pulled out his map he created, and looked at the parts around the lake. "There. Let's go east!" He continued, pointing in the direction he wanted to go.

The two walked around the lake in silence, Rina sulking at the thoughts going on in her head. Aiden tried to stay positive and get her involved in the exploration of the woods. The two walked for a while in the same direction. They only stopped when Aiden thought it necessary to leave some sort of mark they could use to find their way back. He used his dagger to carve an arrow in trees, pointing them in the direction to the lake, then wrote them down on his map with the marking where they were.

"What do you think is out here?" Rina asked.

"I don't know. Dad said that past the lake was where the first war had been. Maybe we'll find some old weapons or something from the war." Aiden replied, ducking a branch. "Probably, we won't find anything and will have to head back."

"I hope that boar doesn't come back." Rina said, scared of what would happen if they got attacked again.

"Don't worry, we will be ok..." Aiden reassured, getting distracted as the two walked into another clearing. Both stopped and stared at a shack resting in the center of a small field. "It looks abandoned."

"I... I don't want to go in there Aiden..." Rina stated, grabbing onto his arm, hiding behind him. "It looks scary."

"It's probably empty." Aiden replied as he scribbled the shack's location on his map. "It looks like no one has been there in years. We might find something cool inside, aren't you curious?"

"A little... But it looks scary!" Rina continued to emphasize the scariness of the shack. "What if there's a monster inside?"

"There's no such thing as monsters Rina." Aiden comforted. "Here, stay by the tree, I'm going to go look in the windows and see if I see anything or any sign of life, then we will decide to go in or not. Sound good?"

"Okay. Be careful!" Rina said, hiding behind the tree.

Aiden quietly crept towards the shack, agreeing in his head that it did look creepy. Cobwebs hung from the shingles down to the walls, giant spiders resting in the middle. The stone that made the walls were cracked all over, looking as if the house could crumble at any moment.

Aiden reached the dust covered windows, using his sleeve to wipe away the grime so he could see inside. Squinting, Aiden was unable to see much, there was no light coming from within the shack. "It looks..." Aiden started to say when he felt something touch him.

Slowly turning his head, Aiden saw a massive spider resting on his shoulder, staring at him. "Ahhhhhh!" He screamed, using his hand to swat the spider off him as he ran back towards the trees where Rina sat on the ground laughing at him.

"That's not funny!" Aiden yelled at Rina, shaking his body, feeling as if there were a hundred of them still on him. "I hate spiders..."

"There's none on you." Rina consoled. "You got them all."

"Come on, it's safe. There's nothing but spiders..." Aiden replied, grabbing her hand, pulling her towards the shack.

The two slowly cracked open the front door, peeking inside to see if there was any form of life. Everything was quiet within, there were no sounds, not even that of vermin. Aiden pushed the door completely open, listening as it creaked the whole way. The cabin only had one room that was covered in dust.

Aiden could make out what looked like a stove in the far corner of the room, and what looked like a desk resting not too far from it. There were books and papers all over the desk, none of which the two could read. "It looks like it's in another language." Aiden commented, dropping a book back down.

While Aiden was looking around the desk, Rina found a bed with a wooden chest at the end of it. As she opened it, the chest creaked the same as the front door. "More books." Rina stated as she dug through the box, looking for anything interesting. "This book... It says magic on it." She continued, holding the book up.

"Let me see." Aiden replied as she handed the book to him. It was a leather-bound book sealed with a latch. "It's... rusted... shut..." Aiden stated as he struggled to pry open the fastener, wanting to see the contents of the book.

Using all his might, Aiden finally pulled open the book, falling backwards as the latch gave way. Rina giggled as she watched the book drop to the ground with her brother. She picked up the book as Aiden got back to his feet and opened it to find out it was hollow inside with only a necklace resting within. "What is that?" Aiden questioned, looking down into the book with his sister.

"I don't know." Rina answered, shrugging her shoulders. "It looks like a necklace. But the gem..." She continued, poking the stone resting in the locket. "It's not shiny."

"I wonder why someone would put a necklace in a book." Aiden stated, walking back towards the desk. "Are you going to keep it?" He asked, as he opened the drawers, hoping to find something useful.

"I think so. I like it." Rina replied, putting the jewelry around her neck and hiding the gem under her shirt. "Have you found anything?"

"No." Aiden sulked. Tossing more papers on the ground. "It's all useless."

"It's getting late, Aiden. We should get back home." Rina told him, as she looked out the window and saw that the sun was starting to set.

The two walked quietly through the woods. Aiden's mind went back to how his sister summoned so much fire and had it contained. He wondered how she did not notice what she had done, how she had been so focused on concentrating that she did not feel the heat from the flames.

It scared him, something that he would never tell her, but the power she has worried him. He wants her to be safe, but also wants her to be able to control the magic. He felt that it was his responsibility to keep her safe from everything. Looking over at Rina, he saw that she was playing with the gem of the necklace, staring at it. "You can't tell mom or dad about that."

"Why not?" Rina asked.

"They're going to ask where you found it." Aiden said bluntly. "Then there will come more questions, and then they may find out about your magic. We don't know how they will react. It's better if we figure this out on our own for now."

Rina nodded, understanding how protective their parents were. She didn't want to worry them any more than they already seemed to be. As far back as she could remember, Rina always felt that they worried, specifically about her.

She felt that everything she ever did was watched closely by both of her parents. Sighing, she took the jewelry off her neck and slid it into her pocket as the two of them came out of the woods with their home in sight.

Chapter 4

Erik stared at the sky, lost in his memories. Thoughts of the war haunted his mind, seeing the faces of the people he killed in the name of the King. It was not only the lives his hands took, it was also all the lives the weapons he created stole. He knew that out of everyone in the war, he was responsible for the most deaths.

He had never thought of such a life when he was younger, only wanting to work with his hands, making tools, and protecting those who were important to him. Turning his gaze from the clouds above, Erik saw his goal in the distance.

"There it is Ellie!" Erik exclaimed, happy to see his destination. "Osion." Osion was a small village, having a few dozen homes, one inn, and a tavern towards the center of the town. Their main source of trade was fruit and meat from the farms that sat on the outskirts of Osion.

Ellie barked excitedly, jumping off the seat to run in the fields leading to the village. Erik watched Ellie run around happily as they neared Osion, smiling to see how joyful she was. "Come on Ellie! We will have more time for running around later."

Erik steered the wagon towards the center of the village where he knew the trader, Terran, lived, bought, and sold supplies. He had done business with the man for years, Terran continuously gave him a fair price and always had information about what was going on in Kaskia and Premus.

"I wasn't sure I'd see you this season." Terran commented as he held the door open for Erik. "You too, Ellie." He continued, petting Ellie as she trotted through the door.

"It's been a rough year, I haven't had a lot of chances to make my way out here." Erik replied, dropping the sack of supplies that he brought. "How have you been?"

"A rough year indeed." Terran agreed. "Tension is building again. Every few weeks there's Kaskian soldiers in the area. I haven't seen any trade coming from Premus in the last few months too."

"That's not good." Erik replied, knowing that the only reason for trade to stop, is if war was coming. "Will this be enough for the usual supplies for the winter?" Erik continued, gesturing to the gear he dumped onto the counter.

"Let's see." Terran answered, checking the items that Erik brought. "As always, beautiful work. I still don't get why you make a living making these items when you could go to Dealay or Toogal and make a good living making weapons and armor. But yes, this will do."

"As always, that is not a life I wish to live. I enjoy what I have." Erik retorted. "Do you mind helping me to load the wagon?"

"Not at all." Terran answered, setting the supplies he got from Erik in the back room. "How long are you in town for?"

"I hope that we can get back on the road soon. I would like to be home before the weeks over." Erik replied, picking up a sack of fruit, slinging it over his shoulder. "It looks like a storm is coming, in more ways than one, and I would like to be nowhere near it."

"It does." Terran agreed, picking up another sack of supplies. "The weather has been pretty bad lately."

A woman's scream cut their conversation short as she came running down the road yelling for help. Ellie growled, looking in the direction of the shriek. Erik dropped the bag of food and pulled out his sword. "Terran."

"Already with you." Terran replied, grabbing a sword that had been resting on the inside of his door.

A barefooted woman came running towards the two, covered in dirt and mud, looking as if she had fallen while running from whatever scared her. "They're in my house and destroying everything!" She cried as she ran into Terran's arms.

"Who are they?" Terran asked.

"Where are they?" Erik added.

The woman pointed in the direction that she came from. "Bandits..."

Erik tightened his grip on his sword and ran in the direction of the bandits, Ellie and Terran on his heels. In only minutes, the trio arrived at the woman's house. The door was torn off the hinges and tossed in the middle of the road, broken in two. Ellie growled, her hair on edge, ready for any threat to come out of the house.

"Look what we have here!" A man yelled, glancing out of a broken window of the house. "We got some do gooders!"

"Be ready." Erik stated to both Terran and Ellie.

A large man walked out of the house, kicking aside what was left of a broken desk. Behind him, followed a half-dozen, smaller men, all armored in rusted and ragged chainmail that rattled when they walked. The large man carried an even larger hammer resting on his shoulder, a hammer that he seemed to carry with ease. All his bandits wielded varying sizes of swords or daggers. "What do you want, little man? We're busy!"

"Leave this place and its people alone!" Erik replied.

"And what if we don't? Little man!" The large man mocked. "Are you going to tickle us with that toothpick of yours?"

Without giving Erik and Terran a chance to reply, the large man gave the signal for his bandits to attack. Like ants to a picnic, the bandits swarmed around the trio, all laughing and mocking their opponents, underestimating the skills based on their looks. All the bandits saw was an old man, a little dog, and a traveler who did not belong.

Ellie barked loudly, surprising the bandits at the ferocity, giving Erik the opportunity to attack first. Catching a man off guard, Erik landed the hilt of his sword against the man's face, knocking him out with the force of the attack. The remaining five bandits roared in anger, only to have another fall to an attack by Terran. Neither Terran nor Erik wanted to slay the bandits, that was not the type of men they were. "Four left. Who's next?" Erik taunted.

Where they once had the trio surrounded, the four remaining bandits now stood together in front of their enemy. Ellie was the first to attack the remaining four. Jumping straight at one of the men, knocking him off balance, pinning him to the ground, barking and growling in his face. One of his comrades tried to help get her off him but was met by Erik and Terran together, Erik kicking the man in the gut, Terran coming up after with the flat side of his sword slamming into the man's face, sending him stumbling backwards.

"No more games!" The large bandit leader yelled. Slamming his giant hammer in a downward arc at Ellie, missing by an inch, only to squish his subordinate. The leader was quick for his size, while his hammer rested in the stomach of his fallen comrade, he kicked Terran in his chest, sending him flying backwards. "You're next little dog!"

"No! You face me!" Erik yelled, charging at the large man. He swung his sword in an attempt to wound the bandit, only to miss as the large agile man side stepped and used a giant armored hand to hit Erik in the back of the head.

"Get the dog!" The leader yelled to the two remaining bandits.

"How about you try to come after me?" A voice taunted the bandits.

"A Felien..." The bandit leader spat. "You're an abomination of the king!"

Erik got up to see the leader and the two remaining bandits charge at their new opponent. The Felien wore leather armor and moved far faster than the bandits could keep up with, he had black short fur that showed where there was no armor. The Felien ducked the giant man's hammer and ran after the two smaller men, landing a powerful punch to the chest of one, sending him sprawling backwards, then grabbed the second by the face and slammed him into the ground, leaving only the giant man with his hammer.

"Is that all you bandits got?" The Felien taunted.

Without letting the battle go on any more, Erik charged the leader, landing a well-placed hit with the hilt of his sword square on the back of the man's head, knocking him unconscious.

"Why did you do that?" The Felien asked. "I wasn't done playing with him yet."

"I know you could have finished him with ease." Erik answered, holding his sword towards the unarmed Felien. "What are you doing here? Your kind never leaves the capital without a reason."

"You got me." The Felien replied. "My name is Kerd, and I've been sent, by King Cladon, to investigate the bandit activity in the area and squash the threat to the people of the land."

"Then you're done here." Erik replied, with Ellie by his side, growling. "You can go back and report your findings."

"I mean you no harm." Kerd replied, his hands raised in the air. "I'm not done here yet. I need to find out where they came from and why they're here."

"Then figure it out and leave Osion." Erik replied, backing towards Terran to check on him. "Are you alright?"

"I'm... I'm okay. I'm not as young as I used to be." Terran replied as he stumbled to his feet. "What did I miss... Is that a Felien?" He asked, pointing to Kerd who was kneeling over the bandit leader, poking him in the belly.

"Yes. I don't trust him. He says he was sent by the King to investigate the bandits." Erik replied.

"I can hear you, you know?" Kerd interrupted, standing up. "Fine. Fine. I will leave. I got all I need from these bandits." He continued, waving a furred paw as he walked out of Osion.

"I need to go; will you be able to handle getting rid of these guys?" Erik asked, pointing to the group of unconscious bandits.

"We will be fine. We don't have any fighters here, but we do have plenty of people willing to move these bandits away from our town." Terran replied, shaking Erik's hand. "Thanks for helping with them. I don't know what we would have done without you."

"Ellie! Let's go!" Erik yelled, as he tossed the second bag of supplies in the back of the wagon. Ellie barked, still anxious from the bandit attack, she stood guard on the wagon, ready for anything.

Erik and Ellie left Osion, the horses leaving a trail of dust behind them as they traveled on the dirt road. Erik wondered where the Felien was, thinking for sure he would have seen the creature on the road by now. Osion was in the middle of a large field, he knew if he did not see the Felien, it was because he did not want to be seen, which made his anxiety worse.

Paranoia crept into his head, wondering if the Felien knew who he really was, if he had overheard Terran and him talking in the shop. All he knew was that he needed to get home as fast as he could, if Cladon knew where he was, his family would be in grave danger.

Chapter 5

"Are you ok Ellie?" Erik asked, petting her on the head, only receiving an agitated bark in return. Erik knew it was not towards him, it was due to the fact that they were attacked. Ellie was still anxious about the battle, she was alert and sensed everything around her. She heard squirrels in the bushes, causing her ears to perk up, just to go back down when she realized what the sound was.

Ellie was searching for the sounds of metal, armor, and the clanking sounds that came with the people who wore such gear. She sat on the seat of the wagon next to Erik, head darting back and forth, left to right, ears perking up and settling back down for the remainder of the day. The sky was blocked by the tree's above them. As the sun set, the life of the woods grew bleeker. Knowing that he would never make it through the woods in the dark, Erik decided to stop the wagon and set up camp for the night.

Erik pulled the wagon off the road and into a small clearing, leaving the horses tied to the carriage, and placing a block of wood under the wheels so it could not move. Ellie jumped off the wagon and searched the nearby woods, making sure there were no enemies around their camp.

Erik went to the back of the wagon and pulled string and cans out of a sack, tying them together and then to trees around the perimeter. Giving him some peace of mind that he would hear someone coming, or at least knowing Ellie would hear it first and alert him to the threat. This was the usual routine that Erik and Ellie had whenever they were camping outside on a trip.

Feeling that the camp was secured, Erik and Ellie made a small fire, sat down together, and ate some jerky that they got from Terran. "Taste good doesn't it Ellie?" Erik asked, petting her on the head. Getting a yip of happiness from her as she devoured the meat. "It's getting late, let's try to get some sleep." Erik commented as he tossed dirt on the fire, extinguishing the flame. He climbed in the back of the wagon, rolled out blankets, and laid down for the night with Ellie curled up at his feet.

Erik was restless all night, nightmares of the past haunting his sleep. Memories of the war, the people he killed, and those he watched die. It had been nearly twenty years, yet the nightmares continued as if it were the previous day. He was scared that the King would come after him for deserting during the war.

A blacksmith of his level that was also a skilled warrior was of short supply. He had heard that the King was furious that he had lost one of his most prized possessions. Something that fueled Erik to leave, the King was mad and sought strength. Cladon cared not for who was harmed on his crusade of power.

The sound of Ellie barking stirred Erik from his nightmares, covered in sweat. "What is it girl?" He asked, trying to focus on his surroundings. He stumbled out of the wagon, sword in hand, Ellie stood just outside, still barking madly. "Who's ever there, come out! Your cover is blown!"

"Very good little man!" The bandit leader replied, stepping out from the bushes with his ragged group. "Your dog is very troublesome."

"What do you want?" Erik replied, pointing his sword at the man. "We don't have anything worth your time."

"But you do. We were told to find someone, and I believe it's you. So, here we are little man." The leader replied, hefting his giant hammer in his hands. "We will take you alive, do not worry. Can't say the same for your little dog."

"Watch my back Ellie." Erik told her, tired of the games, he charged the group. This time, he did not hold back. The six bandits met Erik head on, one after another, they swung their swords. Slicing or stabbing at Erik, and one by one, Erik dodged, sidestepped, or ducked all of them.

Erik was fueled with ferocity, he needed to end this and end it quickly. Their cover was blown, which meant his wife and children were in danger. Each time he dodged their attacks, Erik punished them, breaking their legs, hitting them over the head, or wounding them too much for them to continue.

It was only a matter of minutes before it was just Erik and the bandit leader. This time, the leader was at a loss for words. It was Erik who broke the silence. "Tell Kerd that he will be next if he comes after me." At the words that Erik knew who his boss was, the leader was stunned.

"How did you..." Was all he managed before Erik was upon him. A slice to the back of his leg caused the giant man to fall to one knee. "How can you be this quick... You were nothing yesterday..."

The bandit leader muttered as Erik picked up the hammer and used it against his head.

"Let's go Ellie."

"Stay close by, dinner will be done soon." Brittany told Aiden and Rina as the two ran towards the woods.

"Yes mom!" The two replied.

"Here, take this." Aiden said, handing his dagger to Rina. "You should learn how to wield a weapon and not just rely on magic."

Holding the dagger in her hand, Rina looked at it as if it was something she had never seen. Thinking about the magic that she had been learning to control, she thought about what it would be like to need to use a weapon, scared of hurting anyone. "I... I don't know Aiden."

"It's in case you ever need to, you will be able to defend yourself." Aiden replied, pulling out another dagger from his belt. "Hold it like this, how does it feel?"

"I thought it would be heavier." Rina admitted, turning the dagger over and looking at the craftsmanship. "Did daddy make this too?"

"Yes. He's made all the weapons I have." Aiden answered, while he looked around the bushes nearby. "Here we go!" He said triumphantly.

"What are you doing?" Rina asked, looking over his shoulder curiously.

"We're going to practice." Aiden replied, tossing a small sturdy stick to his sister. "We can't practice with the daggers, we might hurt each other. So, we use these."

Rina placed the dagger by a tree stump and held the stick the way her brother told her to hold the weapon. Aiden showed her how to stand when waiting for an opponent to attack and how to react when an enemy attacked with an overhand, side swing, stab, and multiple other types of strikes.

At first the two trained in slow-motion, giving Rina the time to learn the different reactions. Rina failed many times before eventually picking up how to defend herself. Before they knew it, Rina and Aiden were practicing at normal speed. Aiden would swing his stick at Rina and she would deflect it or dodge the attack. Aiden was impressed with her natural reaction, he knew if she practiced as he did that she would be as good as he was if not better since she has the use of magic on her side.

(A Wizard Warrior...) He thought in awe, imagining how incredible it would be to see someone using weapons and magic as one on the battlefield, plowing through enemies left and right.

"Dinner!" Brittany yelled, snapping the kids out of their training.

"Coming!" The two replied in unison, covered in sweat.

"What have you two been up to? You're drenched!" Brittany chided. "Go clean up!"

Aiden and Rina returned to the kitchen a few minutes later, washed up and ready to eat. Brittany had already laid out their food on the table, from what Aiden could tell, it looked like deer meat and potatoes that they grew outside the house. Aiden dug into the food, always hungry after training. Rina, however, sat there playing with her food, lost in thought.

"Rina?" Brittany asked. "What's wrong?"

"I miss daddy." Rina replied, a frown showing across her face. "How long til he comes home mommy?"

"I miss him too sweetie, and he should be home, hopefully tomorrow or the day after." Brittany answered, smiling at her daughter.

"Mom?" Aiden asked. "Are there any abandoned homes in the woods?"

"Probably. Why?" Brittany answered between bites of her deer meat. "Did you find one?"

"Yeah." Aiden answered truthfully, glancing at Rina. "We were exploring on the other side of the lake and found a creepy shack covered in cobwebs."

"Did you guys go inside?" Brittany questioned, placing her utensils down, staring at Aiden.

"No." Aiden lied, afraid how his mother would react. "I wanted to, but I didn't think it looked safe."

"Good." Brittany replied, leaning back in her chair. "There are a lot of homes that are probably in these woods. If I'm not mistaken, the second war pushed people from their homes in this area, anyone who didn't want to live in Kaskia were forced to abandon their homes and cross the river."

"Do you think there is anything valuable in them?" Aiden questioned. "Any trinkets or armor?"

"It's very possible dear." Brittany answered after taking a sip of her juice. "Why do you ask?"

"I'm just curious what could be in that house." Aiden answered.

"There were rumors that a wizard lived in these woods, back before the second war." Brittany stated. "I suppose, if that was his home. Then yes, there could be something of value in it."

"What are trinkets, mommy?" Rina added, wanting to know more about her necklace.

"Trinkets." Brittany said, thinking on how to answer a difficult question. "Trinkets can be used in many ways. It all depends on the wizard and their intentions.

They could be for protection, they could be a trap to guard something, or they can be used to store magic until a later point, kind of like restoring your energy when you're tired. It really can be anything, anything the wizard can think of and come up with the right spells to work their magic."

"That sounds dangerous." Aiden said.

"It can be." Brittany replied. "That is a reason there's not that many known wizards. People tend to overdo it and pay the price with their lives in the end."

Both Rina and Aiden traded worried glances before finishing their food in silence, not having any other questions that they wanted answers to. Brittany took their quietness as a sign their curiosity was sated, having nothing left to add, she got up to wash the plates they used, leaving the children to get ready for bed. Rina and Aiden gave their mother a hug and said goodnight, having a lot on their minds when they went to sleep, their dreams filled with thoughts of magic and wizards.

Looking down, Rina saw her hands trembling, she felt a cold shiver run down her body, knowing what was about to come. Glancing to her left, she saw someone she could not see their face, but knew that within the armor was her brother, holding a shield in one hand and a sword in the other.

On her right, Rina saw a woman, someone she thought she knew, but had never seen before. The women had long black hair, tied in a ponytail, and wore similar armor as Aiden. She had a shield resting on her back and a sword that looked far too heavy for her, in its sheath.

Ahead of them, Rina could see an army of soldiers, all wearing similar armor as the mysterious women, and carried varying types of weapons from one-handed maces, spears, lances, swords, to giant two-handed hammers.

The sound she had been waiting for finally filled the air, a horn signaling that it was time to attack. Rina reached down to her hip, pulling two daggers from their resting place, and ran alongside the army, unsure who they were or who they were attacking.

Rina heard the woman next to her yell "Shields up!" as a volley of arrows blocked out the sky above, raining down upon them. Raising her hand, Rina summoned a barrier that spread out above her and the soldiers nearest her, protecting them from the onslaught of arrows.

In the distance she heard metal hitting metal, followed by the screams of the dying. While the barrier protected them, Rina used her other hand to summon fire, pinpointing every arrow that was falling from the sky, turning them all to ash before they could cause any more harm.

Rina's head became fuzzy as their enemies came into sight. Most of the opposing forces were that of regular soldiers who dawned plate armor and colors of their nation. The rest were a blur, a moving figure that she could not see any features besides they towered over the bulk of the soldiers they ran beside.

The blurs destroyed the ranks of soldiers ahead of them. Seeing the strength of these creatures, Rina raised both hands into the air, grabbing on an invisible string, focusing all her strength, pulling down from the sky lightning bolts that struck down all of the blurred enemies within range, giving her comrades space to push forward.

Water dripped from above, landing in Rina's hair as she fell to one knee, the spell taking more from her than she thought it would. Rain began falling from the sky, drenching the battleground as the inhabitants of the land fought each other. The world around her began to darken, sounds of battle fading into the distance. Rina could feel her energy draining from her.

She began to panic, searching her thoughts for the source of her dismay, time slowed as her anxiety worsened. A drop of water dripped from her bangs, she watched as the drop of water fell slowly to a puddle in the dirt below. Her mind raced as she saw her reflection in the pool of water, seeing an older version of herself. (Am I dreaming?) He thought.

Chapter 6

Rina sat down, legs crossed, facing the lake. She focused as she had done many times before, remembering the encounter with the boar, seeing its face in her mind, her eyes closed, she remembered the smell, the drool dripping from its mouth. Feeling calm, Rina opened her eyes, concentrating on a part of the water that rested in front of her.

Slowly the water began to steam as a small ball of fire was being created just above the surface. Rina fixated on the flame, holding it at the size of her fist, watching it blaze just above the water, then releasing the flame back from where it came, causing the water to become calm again. Over and over, Rina practiced this technique, wanting to perfect it, for hours, she continued, each time the magic seemed to flow from her faster and easier.

Aiden watched in amazement between his sparring with imaginary opponents. Rina was mastering her ability to control the fire. It had only been a few days since the boar attack and now she was able to hold a flame in the air. He watched as the fire danced over the water when a thought occurred to him on another technique she could attempt. Excited to try, Aiden ran towards Rina. "I have an idea!" He yelled.

"Huh?" Rina replied, turning to face her brother. "What?"

"Hang on." Aiden answered, looking at the ground around him, gathering more rocks into a pile by Rina. "This." He said, holding up a rock triumphantly, showing it to Rina.

"It's a rock." She said confused, poking the rock in his hand.

"Yes." Aiden agreed. "Can you hit it if I throw it over the water?"

"I... I don't know." Rina answered, staring at her hands and then the rock. "I can try."

Aiden gave her a minute to focus, then asked if she was ready to begin, receiving a nod in return. Aiden aimed his rock into the air, throwing it as high as he could so that the rock would end up falling not too far in the distance. Rina watched the rock, focusing on it as she had done when she practiced summoning the fire above the water.

The rock soared upwards, it felt like forever that it went into the sky. Rina waited, waiting for it to fall back towards the water. The rock began its descent, she waited, thinking it was out of her reach, waited and waited, she closed her eyes and released her power. Aiden watched as a ball of fire erupted where the rock had been only seconds before. Rina opened her eyes as she heard the rock splash into the water.

"I missed." Rina sulked, hoping that she would have been able to hit the rock.

"It's ok." Aiden comforted. "It was your first try and you were close. You almost had it." He continued, picking up another rock. "This time, try to aim where it's going to be, not where it is."

Again, Aiden asked if she was ready only to receive another nod. He threw another rock into the air as he did the first. Again, Rina waited for the right time to strike, and again, she missed. Aiden reassured her that she did better and to keep trying. Rock after rock, Aiden threw them into the air, each one Rina was getting closer to hitting with her fireball.

Aiden asked if she wanted to take a break, determined, she shook her head and pointed into the air, signaling him to throw another rock. (I will get it.) She thought as she watched another rock fly into the air. She focused hard, watching its path. She imagined the rock falling faster than it was. Imagining where it will be. "There." She muttered, staring at the spot she knew it would be. Summoning her magic, Rina engulfed the rock in fire as it passed the spot she focused on, destroying the rock, sending rubble raining down to the water below.

"You did it!" Aiden cheered, amazed at the power of the fire she had summoned. He had expected her to hit it, but not destroy the rock.

Rina sighed in relief, happy that she had managed to hit a moving target. "I need a break." She said as she plopped down on the grass, exhaustion taking over. "That was awesome!"

"Are you okay?" Aiden asked, sitting on the grass next to her.

"I'm okay." Rina replied, resting her arms over her knees as she stared into the distance. "Do you ever have weird dreams?"

"All the time." He answered while using a stick to draw in the dirt in front of him. "Sometimes there's flying monsters that are fighting each other, other times, it's just exploring the world and finding treasures."

"I've been having dreams about fighting." Rina stated never breaking her gaze away from the lake. "You were in the one last night, before there was some lady, and she was in it last night too."

"It's probably just from all the magic and training." Aiden replied as he tossed the stick into the lake. "Your mind just has fighting on it and is affecting your dreams."

"Brittany!" Erik yelled as he hopped off the cart.

"What's wrong dear?" Brittany replied, running out of the house to see her husband digging through the bags in the cart.

"We need to leave!" Erik answered, as he calculated how much food supply he had in the cart and how much he needed to retrieve from the house, along with weapons and other supplies. "They found us! We got ambushed in Osion and on our way back. There was a Felien there too. Where are the kids?"

"They... They're out by the lake." Brittany stuttered, knowing what it meant that a Felien was there.

"You need to go get them." Erik told her, grabbing her by her shoulders to get her to focus, knowing how scared she was for her family. "Take Ellie and get them. I will get things ready here, we don't have much time." He continued, hugging his wife and kissing her.

Brittany nodded, understanding what she had to do as she ran back inside to pick up her bow, quiver, and a pouch before running towards the lake with Ellie. Erik watched as they ran into the woods, praying that he managed to get far enough ahead of Kerd to get his family to safety. Once Brittany and Ellie were out of view, Erik went to the forge to grab his sword and shield, placing the latter on his back.

"Ellie, find Aiden and Rina!" Brittany told her, receiving a bark of understanding in return. Brittany knew it would take a few minutes to get to the lake and hoped that her children were there and not off exploring. (Almost there...) She thought to herself when Ellie suddenly stopped in her tracks, hair standing on edge, turning to face their right, growling as she stood her ground.

As soon as Ellie had stopped, Brittany had her bow in hand and an arrow nocked, ready to go. Her training returning to her, she saw her enemies that were hiding in the woods as Ellie smelled them. Not waiting for an invite, Brittany released the arrow, hearing a scream only seconds later. Within an instant, she let loose another arrow, again, followed by another scream.

Then she heard what she had been waiting for, the sound of the leader giving the signal to charge. Kaskian soldiers came running from the woods, more than two dozen emerged with a Felien as their leader. The soldiers raised their shields, charging straight for Brittany, unaware of Ellie.

Ellie ran between the soldiers, biting ankles and arms, going after any weak spot she found, causing each soldier to falter as she moved on to her next prey. Each soldier that she distracted, was met with an arrow from Brittany. One by one, they wounded and slowed their enemies.

The duo fought with ferocity that the soldiers had never seen before. She knew that they were still outnumbered and could not defeat them all, Brittany reached into her pouch and tossed a smoke bomb, once she had reduced their numbers enough to make it harder for them to catch up to her and overwhelm them. "Ellie!" She yelled as she bolted through the woods in the direction of the lake.

"Did you hear that?" Aiden asked. Turning in the direction of their home. "It sounds like fighting..."

"I don't hear anything." Rina replied, turning to look in the same direction only to hear something she knew all too well, a bark from Ellie. "Ellie!" She yelled excitedly as she started to run towards the sound.

"No!" Aiden yelled, racing behind Rina to stop her. "That's Ellie, but something is wrong. We can't just go running, follow me." Aiden explained, pulling her towards the nearest trees for cover, knowing that as long as they were near the lake, they were exposed to anyone in the area. He was positive that he had heard sounds of fighting, and the sound of Ellie barking confirmed it. Her bark was not her normal bark of excitement, it was the type to scare off an enemy.

Aiden and Rina crept through the woods, watching the direction that they heard Ellie. They heard a couple screams from people that they did not know. Their anxiety rose as they got closer to the sounds. They were worried about Ellie and their parents.

Aiden knew that if Ellie was out here in the woods, that it meant their dad was back, and that someone was attacking them. (Could it be the person who lived at the shack?) He wondered. Both children stopped as they saw Brittany and Ellie dart from the woods in the direction of the lake, their mother shooting arrows behind her as she ran.

"Mommy!" Rina yelled too quickly for Aiden to stop her, covering her mouth with his hand and telling her to stay quiet. Aiden noticed that their mother heard Rina and glanced in their direction. Aiden waited for her to signal to them to either join her or to run away. He knew that his priority was to protect Rina.

As if in response to his thoughts, Brittany let loose multiple smoke bombs, covering the entire area in smoke. Not only blocking her from her enemy's view, but that of her children. Rina whimpered as she began to panic, scared for her mother.

"Run!" Brittany told Aiden and Rina as she was in hearing distance, only saying it loud enough for them to hear and not her pursuers.

"Come on out!" Kerd yelled, as his soldiers surrounded the forge. "There's nowhere for you to go."

Walking out, sword and shield in hand, Erik greeted his enemies. "I thought you were after bandits." He stated, gauging the soldiers that had him surrounded. In front of him stood the Felien, Kerd, six soldiers, with their own shield and swords, three stood on both of his sides. To Erik's left and right stood another six and behind them a dozen archers.

"Oh, I found them." Kerd replied, grinning wickedly. "They served their purpose and look what I have found! I knew you were more than you seemed! Erik!"

"I do not know who you're talking about." Erik replied, raising his shield and readying his sword. "You walked onto my land and threatened me. You will regret that."

Without any further words, Kerd signaled for his men to capture Erik. The soldiers that stood on his left and right charged him. Erik returned the charge and ran straight for the soldier closest to him, using his shield to tackle the man to the ground, only to roll back to his feet and bash another with his shield.

The third soldier was too close to use brute force, the man swung his sword only to be parried with Erik's. Hearing the sound, he knew all too well, Erik lifted his shield in time to deflect incoming arrows from the archers, arrows that were aimed at him and the soldiers he was fighting. Downing two more soldiers, only leaving two left in front of him and the six that were chasing him from behind. Kerd and his guards stood watching over the fight, waiting to see if he could survive.

Erik dropped his sword to grab the shield of the soldier in front of him and sent him sprawling behind him, tumbling into the six that were chasing him. Holding his shield up, he knocked down the last soldier that stood between him and the archers. Erik charged them, blocking and dodging all the arrows that they sent towards him.

He was upon them before the soldiers had gotten back to their feet to continue their charge. One by one, Erik dispatched the archers with ease. They were not trained in close combat. Dropping his shield, Erik picked up one of the fallen archers' bow and quiver and began firing arrows at the remaining soldiers, hitting them in weak spots in their armor, causing them to fall one by one.

"Well done, you live up to your reputation." Kerd applauded. "Too bad it's not enough. Don't worry, though, Cladon wants you alive."

Without response, Erik loosed multiple arrows at Kerd and his guards, all of which were blocked by the shields that the soldiers carried. The soldiers moved together, in unison, towards Erik. Where the others made the mistake of charging and underestimating their enemy, these soldiers were patient and well trained. Erik dropped the useless bow, knowing that he would not be able to hit them, and picked up his shield, slowly walking his way towards the nearest sword on the ground. The soldiers did not charge him, they let Erik pick up a sword, well aware that he was just as dangerous without a weapon as he was with one.

The soldiers split into two groups, three on either side of Erik. Try as he could, Erik was unable to keep eyes on all of them, he knew they were forcing him to make the first move, without any other options, he obliged them.

Swinging his sword in a downward arch at the soldier to his left, coming up short on purpose, knowing the ones behind him would attack as soon as he did. Turning just in time, Erik deflected two strikes with his shield and parried the third, then landing a well-placed kick, sending one of his opponents backwards. Glancing behind him, Erik managed to see the other three soldiers attack, giving him time to roll aside, getting away from being surrounded.

"You really are an extraordinary warrior." Was the last thing Erik heard as he felt something hard hit the back of his head, darkness taking over his vision, his sword and shield dropping to the ground, and his body following only seconds later.

Chapter 7

"Run!" Brittany yelled as their pursuers were catching up. The group ran further into the woods, trying as best they could to put more distance between them and the soldiers.

Try as she could, Brittany could not come up with any scenario where they were not all captured, the only way she could protect her children was to slow them down. She had to trust in Aiden and Ellie to protect Rina. Making up her mind, Brittany halted, pulling both Rina and Aiden into a tight hug.

"Listen, there's not much time." Brittany stated, watching for the signs of their pursuers. "Aiden, you must protect Rina and get away from here."

"No, mom!" Aiden protested, pushing away from his mom. "I won't leave you!"

"Mommy!" Rina sobbed, holding her mother tightly in her arms.

"You have no choice!" Brittany yelled back. "They don't want you, they want your father and me. Our past is catching up with us." She said in a gentler voice. "Ellie, protect them. When I can, I will catch up with you. Please be safe, my loves." She continued, kissing both

Aiden and Rina on their forehead. "Do not go towards the house, go further into the woods, head to the river and go south until you reach Osion. Find Terran when you're there, do you understand?"

"Ye... Yes..." Aiden replied, wiping tears from his eyes.

"Good, now go!" Brittany told them, turning away from them so they could not see the tears streaming down her cheeks.

Both Aiden and Rina reluctantly ran away from their mother, Ellie trailing behind them, protecting their rear. Both children had tears strolling down their face as they ran and ran, not knowing how far or how long would be safe.

Brittany hid behind a tree, arrows nocked and ready to go, tears running down her face, knowing that she may never see her children again. She could hear the soldiers getting closer and closer. She took a deep breath, stepped out from behind the tree, surprising the soldiers, and let loose her arrows. Each one finding their intended target. Yet with each enemy down, there were more coming.

"Halt!" Came the voice from the Felien.

Brittany ducked back behind the tree, glancing out towards the soldiers, waiting for whatever they were plotting.

"Give it up!" The Felien ordered. "You cannot possibly believe you can take us all on."

"Who are you and what do you want?" Brittany demanded from the Felien.

"I am Leaon, and I've been sent to retrieve someone for our King." Leaon replied. "You are to come with us, along with anyone you are with!"

"He's not my King!" Brittany replied, peeking out from behind the tree to fire another arrow at Leaon's head.

"I guess we do this the hard way." Leaon replied, catching the arrow in his paw.

Brittany let loose a few arrows, taking out the soldiers nearest to the Felien before realizing that soldiers were closing in on her. She began to panic as she heard rustling sounds coming from every direction. (I'm surrounded... But how!?) She thought, swearing that she had been paying attention to where they were.

Somehow, they had managed to sneak up on her, something that should not have happened. She turned in time to duck away from one soldier and kick another out of her way. Brittany ran in the direction opposite that her children ran, hoping to lure the soldiers away from them, only turning to fire arrows at her pursuers.

"You're surrounded!" A soldier taunted as more appeared in the woods in front of her, only to get an arrow to the face as a reply.

"Give up!" Another soldier demanded, pointing his sword at her. "There's nowhere to run!"

"Who said I'm going to run?" Brittany replied, letting another arrow fly at the soldier who ducked the shot. Before the man realized it, Brittany was in front of him, swinging her bow down hard across his head, sending him face first into the ground. She slung her bow on her back and picked up the soldier's shield and sword and readied herself for the rest that were heading her way. "I may be out of arrows, but I can still take you all on!"

Brittany turned in a circle, shield and sword ready, as she analyzed the two dozen soldiers that had her surrounded, not one of them daring to make a move against her. "Are you afraid?!" She taunted, trying to make them more nervous. "So many of you and only one of me, and you're afraid! You should be! I will kill every one of you!" Brittany ran directly at a group of the soldiers, who flinched at her assault when she threw her sword at them, missing completely.

The soldiers looked behind them to see the sword sticking out of a tree, before turning back in time to see Brittany holding the shield up with both arms as she plowed through the group, knocking them down.

Once she was out of the circle of soldiers, Brittany retrieved the sword and began attacking the soldiers before they could recover, taking out the nearest ones with ease as the remainder of the two-dozen converged on her. Filled with bloodlust, Brittany parried, blocked, dodged, and countered every soldier that came at her, fending them off as long as she could.

One by one, the soldiers fell to her blade, their bodies piling up around her, giving her an added defense against the oncoming soldiers, causing them to trip over their fallen comrades.

"Enough fools!" Leaon shouted to his soldiers as he walked towards Brittany confidently. His soldiers cleared a path for him as he neared his target. "Pathetic! Over two dozen of you and you cannot capture one little human female!"

"Why don't you try?" Brittany taunted, banging the sword on her shield. "You're not the first Felien that I have faced and defeated!"

"I will not be tricked into petty emotional taunts as these useless fools!" Leaon replied, getting within striking range of Brittany's sword, his muscles rippling as he extended his claws. "Give me your best!"

Brittany obliged the furred opponent, stabbing her sword directly towards his gut, only to miss as Leaon sidestepped the attack with ease. With her foe now standing in front of her shield, she attempted to bash him with it, only to fail as the Felien grabbed the top of the shield with his paw, and yanked it out of her hands, tossing it behind him.

Undeterred, Brittany followed the shield bash with a diagonal slice of her sword, catching the Felien off guard with her ferocity, grazing his bare chest with the tip of the blade and he attempted to back step the attack.

"Enough!" Leaon yelled, placing a paw over his wound, glaring at Brittany who stood with both hands on the hilt of the sword, ready for his next advance. Where he had walked casually towards his opponent previously, Leaon charged towards her this time, ducking her final strike before reaching a long arm past her attack, placing his paw around her neck, lifting her off the ground and pinning her against a tree.

Brittany dropped the sword to grab the beast's arm, struggling to free herself from his grasp. "You will not die this day." He stated before throwing her backwards into the remaining soldiers. "Chain her and go find the others she was with! No more delays or you'll be the ones in chains!"

"No!" Brittany yelled, struggling to free herself.

"Aiden! I can't run anymore." Rina cried, rubbing tears from her eyes. "I'm too tired."

"Come on, Rina." Aiden told her. "We have to go! If we don't stay safe, then they could use us to get to mom and dad. We have to stay strong, they're going to find us! There's no way they can catch our parents, just no way!" He told her, and himself.

"Over there! I heard something" Came a voice from behind them.

Without a word, Aiden grabbed Rina by the hand and pulled her, only to be stopped by Ellie who paused in front of them, her hair standing on edge, growling.

"It's that dog again!" One of the soldiers said as they came from every direction to surround the trio. "Don't get too close to it."

"Rina." Aiden said calmly, pulling out his dagger. "We have to fight. Remember how we've been training and use that against them. Don't hold back, or else they will overwhelm us."

Rina sniffled and pulled out the dagger her brother gave to her. "Ok... Okay."

"Isn't that cute?" The soldier mocked. "They're going to fight us with toothpicks!"

Ellie answered with a bark as she pounced on the man who teased her family. As she tackled the soldier, the other ones nearby charged Ellie to get her off him, only to be met by Aiden, who quickly surprised the first soldier, landing his dagger between his armor, causing the man to stagger backwards, holding his wound.

He then charged at the next soldier, sidestepping a slice from the man's sword, then moving within range to thrust his dagger under the armor and into the soldier's abdomen. As good as Aiden was, the soldiers were better, a third one used his shield to knock Aiden to the ground, standing over him with his sword pointed at his throat, wanting him alive.

"No!" Rina yelled, without hesitating, she summoned a fireball above her hand, thrusting it in the direction of the soldier that held his sword at Aiden's throat, landing directly on his chest. The fireball exploded on contact, sending the man flying into the nearest tree, cracking the trunk on impact.

As if possessed, Rina turned her attention to the soldiers nearing Ellie, doing the same to them as she did the one before, summoning fireballs at her fingertips and throwing them at each enemy. Her aim true, one by one, Rina used her new found magic abilities to take out the soldiers as Aiden lay on the ground, watching in awe.

With each fireball, a soldier flew into trees, causing the forest to echo with bones breaking and trunks cracking. Aiden stumbled to his feet, shouting "Behind you!" to his sister too late to warn her as an archer snuck up behind her, hitting her over the head with a bow, knocking Rina unconscious. Aiden tried to charge the archer only to be met by another shield that sent him back to the ground. There were still too many soldiers for them to fend off.

Aiden watched in horror as Ellie backed her way up against a tree, surrounded by four soldiers who were closing in on her. Growling furiously, she caused the men to hesitate on getting any closer, their shields protecting them and their swords keeping Ellie from attacking. It was only a matter of time before they would be able to capture her too. Aiden turned to see the archer put chains around his sister's wrists.

Tears streamed down his cheek, dismayed as his world was being taken apart before his eyes. His mother was fighting an army to protect them, he had no idea where his father was, or if he was even still alive, his sister lay unmoving on the ground, and his best friend was being surrounded. He had failed them all. Aiden closed his eyes, losing all hope.

Chapter 8

"Get up!" A voice yelled, snapping Aiden from his distraught. "The battle is not over yet!"

Opening his eyes, Aiden saw something he could not believe. The source of the voice did not come from any human, the voice came from what he thought was a light brown bear clad in mail armor. Aiden watched as the bear used his size to overpower the soldiers.

The bear held a giant hammer in both of his hands, a hammer he wielded with ease. After the awe of his savior had settled, Aiden remembered his sister was unconscious behind him. Glancing in her direction, he saw another bear, this one looking far different from the first. Where the first bear had light brown fur, this new bear had purple fur, and from what he could tell, appeared to be a female bear.

The purple bear, however, did not wear mail armor, she wore a leather tunic and pants, wielding daggers in both of her paws, daggers that she used to protect Rina from the soldiers who had previously captured her.

The male bear kicked a soldier in his chest, crushing the man's armor and sending him tumbling backwards just before the creature swung his hammer into another soldier that was trying to keep Ellie from joining the fight. Ellie eyed the creature, unsure what to make of it as she rushed to Rina's side to protect her.

Ignoring Ellie, the remainder of the soldiers, who had been keeping her contained, turned to face the fierce bear, trying to surround him. The bear brought the hammer over his head, swinging it hard in a downward arc, causing the soldiers to dive away to avoid the devastating blow that cracked the ground.

The bear reached down, grabbing the ankle of one of the soldiers who dove away, and slung him backwards into the other soldiers behind him, sending all of them flying backwards into an armored pile of defeated soldiers.

The purple bear fought with more grace than that of the hammer wielding giant. However, she wielded far more physical power than any human, using her strength to stab armored opponents, her daggers piercing the armor as well as the person wearing them, destroying both with a single attack.

She was far faster than that of her male counterpart. With the soldiers being down, that only left archers firing their arrows at the purple creature. She used her daggers to deflect and slice every arrow that was aimed for her as she slowly made her way to the archers.

Once she was close, the archers abandoned their attack, dropping their bows, attempting to flee. The female bear was too fast for them to get very far, she caught up to them, one by one, stabbing them as she passed them, making their end a quick and quiet end.

Before he knew what to do, the battle was over. The purple bear had saved Rina, who still lay unconscious, where the brown bear had dispatched the soldiers around Aiden and Ellie, who was now beside Rina and growling.

"We mean no harm girl." The purple bear said, placing her daggers on the ground in front of Ellie.

"It's ok Ellie." Aiden said, walking towards Rina. "Is she ok?"

"She will be fine." The brown bear said. "But we need to leave now. There's far too many soldiers in the area."

"Do you mind if I carry her?" The purple bear asked. "It will make it faster for us to travel."

"Where are you trying to take us?" Aiden questioned, tightening his grip on his dagger. "Who are you?"

"You can call me Squishy." The brown bear offered. "And she's Grape." He continued, pointing at his comrade.

"We were sent here to warn you." Grape added. "But we were too late. We need to get out of this area before we get surrounded."

"I know of an abandoned shack not too far from here. Will that do?" Aiden asked, unsure what to do in the situation.

"That will do." Squishy replied while marking a nearby tree. "Let's go."

"Aiden!" Rina yelled, searching the battlefield for her brother. She was surrounded by soldiers fighting each other, all of whom paid her no attention as she stumbled the warzone, drenched as rain fell from the sky. She tried to focus on the last thing she could remember, unsure how she ended up in the middle of a battle.

The flow of the skirmish passed around her as if she was a boulder resting in a river. The sounds of fighting echoed across the land, making it harder for her to gather her thoughts. Thunder cracked above her as she saw a bolt of lightning strike down a few paces in front of her. "Aiden!" She yelled again, unsure why she was drawn to where the bolt struck.

Rina pushed herself past soldiers who were gathered in a large ring, the two armies on opposing sides with two combatants at its center. She focused on the two soldiers circling each other at the midpoint of the ring.

Rina watched as the two gauged each other, exchanging words that she could not hear. One was armored from head to toe, wearing armor that glistened in the rain, holding a sword and a shield. She wasn't sure how, but she knew the armored fighter was her brother, the one she was searching for.

Her heart ached as she beheld Aiden's fearsome opponent, a furred creature that resembled a lion to her, who stood taller, more muscular, and scarier than she thought her brother would ever be. Yet, Aiden stood his ground, staring down the lion looking creature, daring it to make the first move.

Voices coming from her right caught her attention, although she could not make out the words. Turning, Rina saw two females talking to each other as they watched Aiden. She swore that she had seen the armored female from somewhere before but couldn't place where.

The other female, who wore a white hooded cloak, had her back towards her, blocking the view of the woman's face. All noise of the war faded, the rain fell silently over the battlefield, she watched as the hooded female slowly turned to face her, gasping as she recognized her.

"It's okay Rina." The hooded figure reassured her. "Have faith in Aiden, have faith that everything will be okay. You must wake up now."

Squishy and Aiden led the group through the woods, the latter checking his map as they traversed the forest, the former holding his hammer tightly in his grip, ready for any threat to emerge from the shadows. Grape followed closely behind them, carrying Rina in her arms and close to her chest, protecting her from any danger that could occur. Ellie followed in the back of the group, alert for any pursuers that would be following them, sniffing the air for any scents.

Aiden held his dagger nervously, trembling with fear of all that had occurred, trying his best to harden his nerves. His thoughts getting the best of him, wanting to help his mother, wondering what happened to his father and why he was nowhere to be seen, and worried about Rina, who was now his main priority. He kept telling himself that he would stay with the bears until she woke up and they figured out what was going on. Although they saved them, Aiden was not ready to just throw his trust into strangers.

"How much further?" Squishy asked quietly as he marked another tree.

"Only a couple more minutes." Aiden answered, looking at the map he had created of the area. "There! In the middle of that field."

"Stay here." Squishy told the group, pointing behind the trees. "Let me check and make sure it's clear."

Aiden watched quietly as Squishy walked confidently towards the shack, first towards the windows, then to the front door, swinging it wide open. After a couple seconds, he exited the house to walk around it, then sent the signal that it was safe for them to follow.

"Now that we're here. Tell me what's going on!" Aiden demanded, as Grape lay Rina on the bed. "What are you two?"

"We are Bermion." Squishy stated. "Grape, get to the roof and keep an eye out for any signs of Kaskian soldiers."

Nodding, Grape left the shack and quietly climbed to the roof, making no sounds as she made her way up.

"We were sent here, as Grape said, to warn you." Squishy continued. "We were not sure who we were warning. Magic was sensed in the area and we were sent here. We knew that Cladon would send his soldiers to come for whoever was here."

"How did you find us?" Aiden demanded, not telling Squishy that it was Rina who used magic.

"This." Squishy replied, pulling out an amulet. "It points us in the direction where magic was used. Magic leaves a residue, something that can be tracked, if the caster is not shielded. Never did we expect someone so young." Squishy stated, looking at Rina.

"Who sent you?" Aiden asked, his head filled with questions.

"You will meet him eventually, for now, we cannot say. For the chance they get ahold of you, Cladon must not know his name and where he is." Squishy answered. "What are your names?"

"I'm Aiden, that's Rina and Ellie." Aiden answered, pointing at Ellie who was staring out the window, fur still standing on edge. "What about our parents? Did you guys see them on your way to us?"

"That was not our mission." Squishy said sadly. "However, we have two companions with us who are searching the area. They will be meeting us here shortly. Maybe they will have good news."

"Aiden..." Rina said, as she woke up rubbing her head. "Where... What is that?!" She screamed when she saw Squishy.

"It's ok Rina." Aiden said, sitting next to her, hugging her tightly.
"Are you ok?" Ellie barked while licking Rina all over her face.

"I'm ok... My head hurts and I had the weirdest dream..." Rina replied, hugging Aiden and Ellie back. "Who... Who is that?"

"That's Squishy. He's a Bermion, there's another one, Grape, on the roof." Aiden answered, pointing above their head. "They saved us."

Aiden explained to Rina what had happened and what he learned from Squishy. Aiden and Rina sat there quietly, both scared of what would happen and what may have happened to their parents. Ellie lay next to them, resting her head on Rina's lap, whimpering as she too worried.

Squishy stood by the window, watching the woods in the distance, glancing back at the children, making sure that they were alright and feeling sorry for the situation that they were thrown into. Squishy's mission was to protect them and he would sacrifice his life to do so, he could see the love they had for each other and wanted to protect them from all harm that Cladon would send after them.

He knew that they were not prepared for such an enemy as Cladon, he knew that he was not prepared for it either, Squishy just hoped that he could get them where they needed to go.

Two thumps from the roof broke Squishy from his thoughts. "They're here." He stated, looking at the ceiling above.

"Who's here?" Aiden asked. Standing in front of Rina.

"Arlington and Jr." Squishy said just before the door opened.

Aiden and Rina both gasped as Grape walked through the door with two fierce looking creatures at her side.

"This is Arlington, and that's Jr." Squishy said, pointing at the two creatures. "They're Kaiine, in case you're wondering."

"And I'm Grape." Grape added, kneeling by Rina. "How are you feeling?"

"I... I... I'm okay..." Rina answered in awe of the new companions.

Aiden stared at the two Kaiine, taking in their appearance. The one who Squishy said was Arlington looked like a wolf with gray and white fur. Jr, looked like a fox with his red fur. Both newcomers wore tunics and cloaks with bow and quivers strapped to their backs, something Aiden felt they did not need to fight. "How old are all of you?" Aiden asked, realizing that all the creatures did not sound like the soldiers, they sounded like they lacked experience and confidence.

"Well." Squishy said. "I'm Eighteen, She's Seventeen." He continued pointing at Grape.

"I'm sixteen." Jr. added. "And he's thirteen." He said, pointing at Arlington.

"You're all young..." Aiden stated. "Barely older than I am."

"We're all Adepts at our skills, well except Arlington, he's still an Apprentice." Grape responded. "We were raised and trained for the battle to come."

Shaking his head, Aiden wondered how a bunch of kids were going to protect them from the King and his army. Wishing his parents were there to help. "Wait!" He said. "Our parents! Did you find them? Are they ok?" Aiden questioned, pleading to the Kaiine.

"They're okay." Jr. sighed. "But they've been captured by the soldiers. There was a Felien with them and their Elite guards."

"No!" Rina cried out, falling to her knees. "It's all my fault!"

Aiden knelt next to her, holding her in his arms as Ellie sat on the other side of Rina. As bad as he wanted to join her and mourn the loss of their parents, for surely, he thought they would never see them again, he had to stay strong for Rina. "It will be ok. We will find them." He reassured her, hoping that his words were true.

"He's right, Rina." Grape added. "We all will help rescue them, I promise."

"Squishy, do you think he will help?" Jr. asked. "We will need both their parents for the battle to come. They were amazing!"

"I'm sure he will. But first we have to get to him." Squishy answered, pulling out a map of Kaskia. "and that's a long journey across Kaskian territory."

"Amazing?" Rina sniffled.

"Yes, amazing!" Arlington exclaimed, punching the air in front of him. "Both your parents took out so many soldiers, more than our whole group could. The only reason they were defeated were those Felien!" Arlington continued, stomping his foot.

"Felien are not to be messed with." Squishy added, seeing the confusion on Aiden's and Rina's face. "There are not many of them in Kaskia, thankfully, but they are far more powerful than any of us."

"More agile too." Grape added.

"I still think that if your parents fought them one on one." Arlington said. "That your parents would have won. I've never seen any humans fight the way they did."

"How do we know they will be safe?" Rina asked, wiping tears from her face.

"From what we know, they wanted you." Squishy stated, pointing at Rina. "I know it's hard to hear, but until they can get you, they will keep your parents safe, so they can try and lure you to them."

(War is like fighting a god of unlimited power. No matter how hard you fight, no matter what and who you lose, war will always be there. The only way to survive and hope to win, is to stay strong, stay focused. Out-smart your enemies. You may not be able to kill a god, but you might be able to banish it temporarily.) Erik's voice echoed in Aiden's mind. (I must stay strong, strong for her, and for them.) He thought.

"Arlington, Jr. Go check and see if the woods are safe for us to leave." Squishy ordered. "We need to get going, will you three come with us?"

Aiden and Rina looked at each other, then they looked at Ellie who barked in agreement with them. "Yes." They said together.

"Can we talk before we leave?" Aiden asked Squishy.

"Yea, Grape stay with Rina." Squishy answered, opening the door for Aiden to walk out first, Ellie following him.

"What's on your mind?" Squishy asked once they were out of earshot from everyone.

"What are we really facing?" Aiden asked bluntly. "What does Cladon want?"

"He wants your sister's power." Squishy sighed. "He wants to take it from her and absorb it into his own, which will sacrifice her life in doing so. He doesn't want anyone else in the world with power that could rival his own."

"How does this person you want to take us to plan to help?" He questioned, fiddling with the dagger in his hand.

"He's very powerful, probably one of the few alive that could stand against Cladon." Squishy explained. "You will understand what I mean when you meet him."

"How far is he from here?" Aiden continued to question.

"A few days, maybe more. It all depends how fast we can travel and if we run into any trouble along the way." Squishy answered honestly.

"It's not going to be easy by any means. Cladon does not know where we're going, but they will be on our trail the whole time."

"Then we need to leave." Aiden stated. "And you all have to protect Rina at all costs."

"I promise, we will protect you both with our lives." Squishy assured. "I believe you two have a very important role in the future of this land."

"It's safe to leave." Arlington interrupted. "Jr. is scouting further that way." He continued, pointing in the direction of the woods behind the shack.

"Then we shall leave now." Squishy said, walking back to the house to get the others.

Chapter 9

Aiden glanced back at the shack, feeling a twinge in his heart at the thought of never seeing his home and parents again. Wiping a tear from his eye, he turned his gaze upwards, seeing sunlight breaking through the trees above, the light brightening the path ahead of them.

Remembering that he was not alone, he steeled his emotions for the sake of his sister and pressed on. He wondered where Jr. was, never seeing the Kaiine, Jr. was always scouting ahead and leaving little symbols marked on trees for Arlington to find, guiding the rest of the group safely ahead.

Squishy was quiet as he walked behind Aiden and Rina, bringing up the rear of the group, listening for any signs of pursuers. Grape stood firmly at his side, watching the children, thinking of what their life may end up like if they failed to protect them.

"We need to train them." Grape whispered to Squishy. "They need to be able to protect themselves, just in case we cannot."

"I agree." Squishy sighed, knowing how much trouble they're likely to run into. "This is not going to be an easy journey."

"What about Ellie?" Grape asked. "She seems very well trained. Do you think we can get her to help protect us while we're traveling?"

"I'm sure she can." Squishy admitted. "But that's something that has to come from them." He said, pointing at Rina and Aiden. "I do not believe she will listen to anyone but them. They're her family and she seems to guard them with her life."

"Where are we going?" Aiden asked Squishy as he slowed down to walk with them.

Nodding to Grape, Squishy replied. "Cosan village. If we're lucky, we will arrive there tomorrow, hopefully before noon."

"Is that where he is?" Aiden asked, watching as Grape caught up with Rina.

"No. We need supplies. We didn't bring a whole lot with us because we were in a rush to get to you." Squishy answered. "The plan was to head there or to Osion, whichever was easiest. Since we are already heading east, Cosan is the village we need to go to, it's on our way."

Aiden nodded his head, understanding what Squishy had told him. He watched as Grape talked with Rina, wondering how his sister felt about the situation, traveling with strangers. Aiden was thankful that they had Ellie with them, she knew a lot and gave him some sense of ease being away from home.

"She's very well trained." Squishy stated, as he looked at Ellie.

"Dad trained her." Aiden told Squishy. "He trained me too."

"Your father must be a very skilled fighter." Squishy stated, patting Aiden on the shoulder. "I bet he is very proud of you."

"I guess." Aiden sulked, thinking that he had failed, that the only reason Rina is safe is because of Squishy and his group.

"May I see your dagger?" Squishy asked.

"Here." Aiden replied, handing his dagger, hilt first, to the Bermion.

"The craftsmanship is amazing on this." Squishy said, staring at the blade and hilt, admiring the balance between the two. "Who made this?"

"My dad." Aiden replied, still watching Grape and Rina.

"Do you mind if I walk with you Rina?" Grape asked as she caught up with Rina and Ellie.

"No." Rina answered, staring at Grape. "I've never seen a Bermion."

"There's not many of us in Kaskia." Grape stated. "How's Ellie?"

"She's okay I guess." Rina replied, looking at Ellie who Barked quietly. "I think she misses home too."

"What's wrong?" Grape asked, stopping alongside Rina.

"This is where the boar attacked us." Aiden answered, as he and Squishy caught up with them. "This is where she first used magic and all this got started."

"Here." Grape said, handing a trinket to Rina. "Keep this on you and no one will be able to sense you when you use magic."

"Thank... Thank you." Rina said gratefully, as they continued walking, placing the trinket in her pocket, where she realized the necklace she had found rested. Rina took out the necklace, placing it around her neck. "You're very pretty, Grape."

"Thank you, so are you Rina." Grape replied. "I see you have a dagger, do you know how to use it?"

"Not really." Rina answered. "Aiden showed me how to defend myself a bit but that's all."

"Here." Grape said, handing Rina another dagger from its sheath. "Don't worry, I have many. If you want, I would like to show you how to use them."

A glimmer of excitement crossed Rina's face as she examined the new dagger, thinking about being as good as her brother, wanting to make him proud of her. "Yes please!"

"Aiden, do you think you can ask Ellie to watch our backs for us?" Squishy asked.

"I can try. It's if she wants to." Aiden admitted. "She always listened to dad, but never us. She does what she thinks is best, I guess."

"Understandable." Squishy said, admiring the loyalty that Ellie had for her trainer.

"Ellie!" Aiden called, receiving a bark back from her as she looked behind at him. "Can you make sure no one sneaks up on us?"

Both Aiden and Squishy looked at Ellie as she kept walking forward with Rina and Grape, waiting for any signs that she understood what he had asked. "I guess not." Aiden sighed. "I'm sure she can sense anything from there though."

"I hope so." Squishy said, handing the dagger back to Aiden. "That's a great weapon. But I think you may do better with a sword."

"What do you mean?" Aiden asked, looking at the dagger he was accustomed to.

"I assume your dad gave you that a few years ago?" Squishy guessed. "Doing so because at the time, that was a good fit for you, as it is for Rina now."

Aiden stared at the dagger, wondering if his dad would feel the same way. "I don't have a sword, and I've never used one."

"If you want to learn how to, we can pick up two swords from Cosan, and maybe a shield if we can find one." Squishy replied. "I can teach you."

"Okay." Aiden said, less enthusiastically than his sister had responded to Grapes offering. Aiden thought about all the times his father had trained him, memories that stabbed at his heart, causing him pain, thinking about never seeing his father again.

Aiden and Squishy continued walking in silence, observing the rear of the group. They watched Grape show Rina how to hold two daggers and how to strike with them as they walked. Aiden's thoughts taking over his mind, how he wished things were back the way they were a couple of days ago. He missed his parents and worried about them, bad thoughts tearing at his head. Aiden didn't even notice that the sun was setting, and the group was almost in darkness.

"There's another abandoned shack ahead." Arlington told Squishy, breaking Aiden from his dismay.

"Then that's where we're staying for the night." Squishy replied. "Jr. already make sure it's safe?"

"Yes, he left a note that all is well." Arlington replied before heading back to the front of the formation.

The group emerged from the woods into another clearing where a cobblestone shack rested in the center. This shack had an oak wooden fence that surrounded the perimeter, and at the front door waited Jr. watched them come out of the woods, tapping his foot impatiently.

"Took you long enough." Jr. said. "I thought you would never make it before dark!"

"Yeah yeah." Arlington replied.

"I'll take first watch." Squishy said. "Aiden, Rina, you two need to get as much rest as you can. It's going to be a long day tomorrow."

"Come inside." Grape said, holding the door for the children and Arlington. Jr. waited outside with Squishy.

"So, Rina, you can do magic?" Arlington asked, curious of what she was able to do.

"I guess, yeah." Rina answered. "Not a lot."

"What can you do?" Arlington pried, wanting to hear more of what she was able to do.

"Can you not ask her so many questions?" Aiden interfered. "She's had a long day."

"Sorry." Arlington sulked.

"It's ok, Aiden." Rina added. "I can summon fire."

"How did you learn to do that?" Grape asked, curiosity chewing at her mind too.

"Hmm." Rina thought. "The first time was because I thought Aiden was going to die when the boar attacked him. I don't know how, I just did it."

Aiden sat by the window, staring at the stars in the night sky, listening to the group while Ellie sat beside him.

"Then Aiden helped me try again." Rina continued, pointing at her brother. "I've been able to summon it easier each time we tried."

"Can you light the wood in the fireplace?" Grape asked, trying to gauge Rina's skill with magic.

"I think." Rina answered, as she plopped to the floor, crossing both her legs, concentrating on the fireplace. In a matter of seconds, a fireball burst to flames in the hearth, destroying the wooden logs that rested there. "I'm sorry!" Rina sulked, thinking that she had done something wrong.

"Don't be sorry, Rina." Grape reassured. "I know what happened and why it happened." She continued, amazed at the power Rina had over fire.

"What do you mean?" Rina sniffled. "What did I do wrong?"

"Nothing wrong. It's a different kind of magic you used." Grape told her. "So far, you've mastered a fireball, it's for fighting. Yes, it's fire, but it cannot be used to light a fireplace, it's more of an explosion than anything else. It's a very powerful and advanced spell."

"That was amazing!" Arlington cheered.

"I can do other stuff than the fireball?" Rina questioned, excited to learn more.

"Yes, and the one we're going to go see can teach you far more than I could." Grape replied. "I can teach you a little about magic, but he can show you stuff I could only dream of."

"Teach me please!" Rina asked, bouncing up and down.

"I will, I will." Grape laughed. "How do you summon the fireball? What do you do?"

"Umm." Rina thought, thinking of her process. "At first, I focused on the boar and the first time I did it. Then I focus on where I want to summon the fire and it just appears."

"That's the problem then!" Grape said triumphantly. "You're focusing on an attack spell for the wrong reasons."

"I don't get it." Rina said, confused as Arlington and Aiden watched closely.

"You've seen a candle or a torch before, right?" Grape asked.

"Yea." Rina answered, still confused, trying to understand what Grape was trying to say.

"Instead of focusing on the boar and how that felt, focus on the flame of a candle, then focus on the fireplace and see if that helps." Grape replied.

Rina plopped down as she always does while concentrating on her magic. She sat on the floor, legs crossed, eyes closed, focusing on the fireplace with the image of a candle's flame in her head. Her mind tried to switch to that of the boar, she fought the urges to repeat what she already knew, the technique she had practiced many times over the past few days. This new technique seemed far more difficult to her, she could feel her forehead sweating, beginning to drip down her cheeks.

"Not again..." Aiden muttered. "Rina snap out of it!"

"What?" Rina questioned, irritated at being interrupted.

"You... You summoned so much fire." Grape said, amazed.

"Wow..." Arlington stuttered, staring at the fireplace, mouth hanging open.

"What was that!" Squishy exclaimed, rushing through the door, hammer in hand, ready for a fight. "Fire burst through the chimney!"

"That happened the first time she focused on the fireball too." Aiden said, helping a confused Rina to her feet. "She summons so much power when she focuses that hard."

"I don't get it." Rina sulked, before glancing at the fireplace, realizing how much soot covered the walls. "I did that?" She continued, tears forming in the corner of her eyes.

"Don't worry Rina!" Grape reassured. "You were amazing! You had it under control. Not even one spark came out of the fireplace!"

"I... I did?" Rina asked nervously, staring at her shaking hands.

"Yes, you did!" Grape replied, patting Rina on her shoulder. "Do not worry so much, your magic feeds on your emotions. Practice and you will have it under control in no time!"

"Go to sleep!" Squishy sighed, as he walked back out of the shack. "And no more fire!"

"Rina, take the bed." Aiden told his sister. "I'll lay on the floor."

Rina laid on the bed without a word, her mind filled with questions. Wondering how she was able to do what she did, how she could control such power. She wanted nothing more than to have her mom and dad walk through the door. Rina rolled onto her side, facing the wall as tears trickled down her face.

She thought about her dreams, curious if she would have another like she has had every night since the boar attack. Everything that went through her mind always changed to memories she had of her parents, hoping that they were safe and got away from the soldiers.

She looked down over the landscape, the wind in her face as they soared over the world. Rina felt free for the first time, a feeling she could not describe in words as she beheld life from the sky. The creature she sat atop roared in excitement, preferring the freedom of the heavens over the cage that it spent an eternity in.

She did not know how she ended up on the back of such a beast, or from whence it came. She only knew that she trusted it with her life. Rina felt connected to it, as if she had known it all her life. Lightning flashed across the horizon, bringing her back to reality. She saw an unnatural fire blazing across the land below, trees covered in the dancing flames, screams of the innocent fleeing their homes.

As if responding to her will, the creature headed in the direction of the screams, hoping that they would be able to help those in need. As they neared, Rina could see a shadow covering the desert, an army of darkness flowing across the ocean of sand.

    Rina sprang from bed in a cold sweat, heart pounding, her eyes focusing on her surroundings. She was once again in the shack, her brother lay sleeping on the floor, Ellie resting at the foot of her bed. The moonlight shone through the window as everyone was sleeping. (Why am I having these dreams? They seem so real...) She thought.

Chapter 10

"What's going on?" Rina asked Aiden, rubbing her eyes as she struggled to wake up and get out of bed. "Where is everyone?"

"Shh." Aiden replied, his ear pressed against the door, listening to Grape and Squishy talking on the other side. "Here they come." He continued, running back towards where he had slept.

"Good morning you two." Grape greeted as she walked into the shack. "There's some berries and bread on the table, once you're done. We're going to head out. Jr. and Arlington are already out scouting the woods to Cosan."

"Thanks!" Rina said, eagerly taking the berries and bread.

"You're welcome!" Grape replied. "If you need anything, I will be outside with Squishy."

"What were they talking about?" Rina grumbled with food in her mouth.

"Magic." Aiden said flatly, getting his gear ready for their trip, taking only a piece of bread to eat. "They're not telling us something."

"What do you think it is?" Rina asked, breaking off a piece of bread for Ellie to eat.

"I'm not sure. Once we're safe, we will ask and demand answers." Aiden said, tightening his belt that held his dagger. "Are you ready?"

Aiden opened the door revealing Squishy sitting on a stump, his hammer resting in his lap as Grape fought an imaginary enemy. Aiden and Rina left the shack, stopping next to Squishy to watch the female Bermion, amazed how Grape fought with such grace and swiftness, almost as if she was dancing. Grape ended her training once she realized that the children were there, ready to go. Squishy explained that there were no signs of Kaskian soldiers in the area, that they seemed to have escaped them, for the moment.

Rina asked Grape question after question about her fighting, how she was so graceful and beautiful the way she fought. Grape thanked her and began showing her some techniques of her fighting style. How to hold the daggers, how to quickly adjust the dagger in her hand to stab backwards when needed. Rina took in every word that Grape said, eager to become just like her.

"How long will it take to get to Cosan?" Aiden asked Squishy, breaking the silence between them.

"At the rate we're going, by nightfall." Squishy replied.

"Are there many Bermion and Kaiine in Kaskia?" Aiden asked, wondering if they would stand out in Cosan because of them.

"There's a few of us around." Squishy answered. "Not so much in the smaller villages, but once we start getting nearer to the capital, there's more. Most Bermion just want to live their lives, Kaiine, they're either for Cladon or against him. That's why Arlington and Jr. will stay out of sight."

"Why doesn't Cladon force any Bermion's in Kaskia to fight for him? He seems to have the power to do something like that." Aiden questioned.

"He probably could." Squishy agreed. "But, to do so, could cause him more harm than the benefit of having us. He is too unsure about us and our homeland to go to war with us while having to deal with Premus."

"What other kinds of magic can I do?" Rina asked Grape, curious of the power she has.

"Well." Grape replied, thinking of the best way to explain it to Rina. "Based off what you have already been able to do, I would say that you will have the ability to use elemental magic. This ranges from summoning explosive fire to calling storms of immense power.

You could potentially have the power over nature, which is extremely rare from what I know. It is always possible that you can learn other kinds of magic too, such as conjuring, manipulation, enchanting, it really is limitless. It's up to the Wizard and what they are able to accomplish."

"What's manipulation?" Rina asked, as her mind raced with the possibilities of what she could do.

"It's the type of magic that lets you control the minds of animals, creatures, and even objects. It usually only works on the simple-minded creatures and animals." Grape explained.

Aiden and Squishy continued walking in silence, listening to Grape and Rina's conversation about magic. The group walked all day, only stopping briefly to rest and eat a small lunch. Squishy promised the children that once they got to Cosan, that they would get a better meal. For hours they walked through what seemed like endless woods.

Aiden saw Arlington twice throughout the day, only when he checked in and gave updates on the surrounding area. Squishy had explained to him that Kaiine are great trackers and scouters, that Jr. usually kept to himself, preferring to always be out scouting alone and has only taken Arlington as his partner when he was ordered to.

"Hey! It's Arlington!" Rina said excitedly, seeing the Kaiine leaning against a tree waiting for them.

"Hi Rina!" Arlington said with equal excitement. "You all are taking too long; the sun is about to set!"

"How far are we from Cosan?" Squishy asked, ignoring the comment from Arlington.

"You're no fun, Squishy!" Arlington sighed. "We're not far. Jr. is already there waiting just outside of town. Shouldn't take but a few minutes or so."

"Let's hurry!" Rina said, eager to see what a village looks like.

"Don't worry, Rina, we will be there soon." Grape replied. "Cosan is a fairly large village and is only getting larger each year. It's the last village in the area that is not full of Kaskian soldiers. Once we go past Cosan, every village and city will have a high presence of soldiers that patrol."

"Yes, so when we're in Cosan, try not to draw any unwanted attention." Squishy added. "Just because there aren't usually any soldiers there, doesn't mean there isn't now. They're on our trail and may already have soldiers positioned in all villages and cities waiting for any signs of us."

As the group neared Cosan, Squishy took out a cloak that was tied around his waist, and wrapped it around him, covering the mail armor that he wore. Grape tucked her daggers beneath her tunic, hiding them from any prying eyes. "We don't need to draw any attention, seeing us in armor and armed would intimidate the villagers and could potentially get the attention of any soldiers in the area." Squishy informed the children who were hiding their weapons from sight.

"There's Jr.!" Rina pointed out as she saw him waiting at the edge of the woods. "That's the village?" She asked, amazed that in the distance, there were buildings that seemed to go on for forever.

"Yep!" Arlington answered, patting Rina on her head.

"Hi Jr.!" Rina greeted as they neared the Kaiine who only nodded in response to her.

"Jr., we're going to go to the Lion's Inn, it's not far from the south side of town." Squishy explained. "After it's dark out, you two join us. Make sure the perimeter of the village is clear of Kaskian soldiers."

The group walked cautiously into Cosan village, Squishy and Grape watching for any threats to the children. Ellie walked near Rina, fur standing on edge, never leaving her side. Aiden and Rina looked in every direction, taking in the sights. They saw people hustling all over.

Aiden made out the sounds of a blacksmith, hearing the constant pounding of a hammer on metal, a sound that pained his heart to hear, reminding him of home and his father that he has not seen in over a day, his father that he hoped was still alive.

As they walked further into the village, he saw traders who had stands on the roads, offering goods of varying types, rugs, blankets, armor, weapons, and many items he had never seen before. As for the people who inhabited Cosan, Aiden noticed that they were almost all human, only noticing a handful of Bermion like Squishy and Grape.

"Is that the Inn?" Aiden asked, seeing a sign, with an image of a Lion above the door.

"That's it is." Squishy answered. "Stay close and don't say anything to anyone."

Squishy led the way into the Inn, a building that had many people inside. It was dark, only a few lanterns resting in what looked like random locations. There were round tables littering the room, people sat around each one, drinking and laughing. No one seemed to notice the group as they traversed the crowd towards the barely lit bar, where a woman was taking orders for food and drinks.

"I need a room for the night." Squishy told the lady who judged the group suspiciously.

"Just one?" She asked, eyeing the children and Ellie. "Why are Bermion traveling with human children?"

"Their parents paid us to get them to Toogal where their grandparents live." Squishy answered confidently. "How much will it be for a room?"

Satisfied with the answer, the woman replied that it would be three dozen gold coins, which Grape took out of her pouch, handing it to the woman.

"Jonathan!" The woman yelled. "Take them upstairs to room six!"

Aiden and Rina looked around the room curious who Jonathan was, seeing a man come from the stairs nearby, a man that disturbed Aiden. There was something off about him. The man was delirious, giggling as he walked towards the group, offering them water that he did not have, which Squishy politely declined, unsure what the man was talking about. They quietly followed Jonathan, listening to his manic giggling while he walked, hearing him muttering to himself.

"Shuch up..." Jonathan told himself as they reached the room where his guests would be staying.

Aiden watched as the man walked back down the stairs, giggling the whole time. "What's wrong with him?" He asked quietly.

"He's delirious." Squishy said, as if that would be enough of an answer.

Squishy closed the door behind them as they entered their room for the night. The room was small, having only two beds, a chair and a desk next to a window that overlooked the road below. Rina and Aiden fell onto the bed, exhaustion taking over, Ellie jumped up next to them, laying at their feet. Grape and Squishy took off their armor and placed their weapons on the desk. "Grape's going to stay with you two. I am going to get some food and supplies for the rest of the journey." Squishy said as he left the room.

"Are you two alright?" Grape asked, seeing how tired they were.

"Yeah." Rina replied.

"We've never traveled this much." Aiden added with a bark of agreement out of Ellie. "What's our next move?"

"We continue on tomorrow morning, we have two options for which way we go." Grape replied. "Which route we take depends on what happens tonight."

"What do you mean?" Rina asked, sitting up to listen to Grape, while Ellie rested her head on Rina's lap.

"We can either start heading north, going more towards the capital." Grape sighed, the tone in her voice indicated this was not the direction she would like to go. "Or we head towards the desert and travel through there. Neither one is an easy task."

"Desert?" Aiden asked, unfamiliar with what she was talking about. "There's a desert near here?"

"What's a desert?" Rina asked, confused.

"Yes, it's massive. No one has traveled across it and returned." She answered Aiden. "And it's an area covered in sand, almost endless from what we know. It's very hot and there's very little out there to survive off."

"Endless sand?" Rina muttered to herself, remembering her dream from the previous night.

"Don't worry. Either way we go, we will be alright." Aiden reassured Rina. "Right Grape?"

"Right Aiden." Grape replied, knowing that he was trying to keep her from getting scared. "You two should try and sleep. It will be a long day tomorrow, and the hardest part of our journey."

Aiden and Rina fell asleep with Ellie laying at their feet. Aiden's dreams were filled with nightmares, reliving the soldiers attacking his family, seeing Rina get hit over the head, being completely useless to help her. He saw his mother fighting the soldiers, getting surrounded and overwhelmed. His nightmare twisted what he knew, seeing his mother being shot with arrows, dozens of them sticking out of her unmoving body.

Aiden watched helpless while his father fought his way to his mother and sister, who both lay on the ground filled with arrows. He tried to run to his father to help but was unable to move. Looking down, Aiden realized that he was bound to a tree. Struggling as much as he could, Aiden was unable to loosen the rope that kept him attached to the trunk. His father blocked, dodged, and parried attack after attack, he was surrounded by an endless army crashing into him the way the ocean does the shore, neither one heeding to the other.

Finding his voice, Aiden called out to his father, pleading for him to get away. The two locked their eyes together just as Erik was overwhelmed by the soldiers who thrusted their swords into him. Aiden watched as his father fell next to his mother and sister, swords protruding from his body.

Aiden sprung straight up as he woke from his nightmare, wiping sweat from his brow. He was greeted by a concerned Ellie who licked his face, reassuring that he was alright. The room was dark, only light shined from the window. Glancing around, he saw that Squishy was back and slept in the chair that was now leaning against the door.

Grape, on the other hand, was nowhere to be seen, Aiden could only imagine that the purple Bermion was hidden somewhere watching over them. He walked over to the window and looked up at the night sky, stars shining bright. He wished that he was back in his room at home, that he could go and hug his parents tightly and never let them go. "What am I supposed to do?" He said softly, tears rolling down his cheeks. "I'm scared."

He turned when he heard Rina tossing in her sleep, wondering what kind of dreams that she was having. Aiden remembered her mentioning that she dreamt of wars and fighting the other day, curious if she was still having them or if they were getting worse. She seemed to be in distress with whatever was going through her mind. Worried for her, Aiden sat next to her, hugging her, trying to calm her mind with a sense of home. He watched as her expression changed from distraught to comfort and peace.

Hearing a noise from the roof broke him from Rina's dreams. He turned to alert Squishy only to be greeted by the Bermion who was already standing behind him, hammer in his hand. "It's ok, it's Jr. or

Arlington, Grape should be with us in a minute." Squishy comforted Aiden.

As he said, moments later, Grape came in through the window. The expression on her face showed that it was not good news. Without a word, Grape moved further into the room, giving space for Arlington and Jr. to sneak in through the window behind her.

"What's going on?" Rina said, rubbing her eyes as she sat up in her bed.

"They're here." Jr. stated. "Kaskian soldiers are in Cosan."

Chapter 11

"How many?" Squishy asked.

"More than five squads of a dozen, each with archers and soldiers." Arlington replied.

"Any Felien?" Grape asked, worried about what their next move was going to be.

"No. Not that we saw." Jr. answered.

"They're coming from the direction of Osion." Arlington added. "If we hurry, we might be able to get out of here without any attention."

"There's too many for our group to slip out of Cosan unnoticed." Jr. said.

"I agree." Squishy sighed. "Alright. Jr., you and Grape take them and head south, towards the desert. Stick to the mission. Arlington, you and I will set up an ambush and slow them down, then we will catch up as soon as we can."

"No...." Rina cried. "You can't leave us!"

"Rina... They have to. They will be okay." Aiden said, trying to comfort her.

"That's what mommy said!" She cried out, tossing herself back on the bed, covering her face in the pillow.

Aiden stood there stunned at the outburst, his heart aching at the words she used. He blamed himself for what happened, and now he knew Rina also blamed him for the loss of their parents. He chose to run away, for all he knew, the three of them staying with their mom may have been enough to save her, then with their mom, they could have saved their father. Aiden played all the what ifs of the day he lost his parents, what could have been.

Ellie nuzzled against Aiden, trying to comfort him, showing that she did not blame him.

"Rina..." Arlington tried to comfort her. "Everything will be okay, I promise. We will be right behind you. But for us all to get away, you have to go with Grape and Jr." He continued, placing his paw on her shoulder.

"Okay..." Rina sulked.

"We have to hurry." Jr. said flatly. "We don't have time for this."

"Here." Squishy said to Aiden, reaching into a bag that he had laying by the door. "I got you a sword. I hope it's not too heavy."

"Thanks." Aiden replied, taking the sword and sheath. Testing the weight of the sword. Although it looked average and nothing compared to the sword his father could make, it felt right in his hand.

"Grape, here's food and supplies for the trip." Squishy said, tossing a small bag to Grape. "We will catch up soon as we can."

Jr. jumped out the window of the two-story Inn, landing silently on his feet. Grape tossed the bag of supplies down to him. "Rina, Jr. will catch you."

"I'm scared..." Rina whimpered, not wanting to jump out the window.

"I will lower you down to him." Grape reassured.

Nodding to Grape, Rina walked over to the window and looked down, seeing Jr. waiting to catch her. Grape picked her up in her arms, slowly lowering her. "I have to let go, Jr. is right there, okay Rina?"

"Ok... Okay..." Rina stuttered as Grape released her grip only to be in Jr.'s arms seconds later.

"Not so bad, right?" Jr. Asked. "Aiden, you're ne..."

Without waiting for Grape to assist him, Aiden jumped from the window, landing next to Jr. and Rina, with less grace than the Kaiine. "I'm fine." He said turning in time to see Grape land right behind him with Ellie in her arms, who immediately jumped to the ground when they landed.

Rina looked up to see Squishy and Arlington disappear on the roof of the Inn.

"Let's go." Grape said.

Jr. led the group as they rushed through Cosan as quietly as they could, dodging anyone who managed to be awake and about in the middle of the night. Aiden, Rina, and Ellie ran right behind him, Grape following behind them, making sure that no one snuck up on them. Jr. suddenly stopped, holding his paw up for them to be quiet. He sniffed the air, then peaked around the corner that they were hiding behind. Ellie gave a low growl. "There's five soldiers and three archers blocking our way out of town." Jr. stated, grabbing his bow and nocking an arrow.

"No other options?" Grape asked.

"No." Jr. replied.

"Aiden, Rina, stay here." Grape told them. "Jr. Ready when you are." She continued, holding her daggers tightly in her paws.

Nodding quietly, Jr. gave the signal to attack. Grape ran around the corner with speed faster than Aiden has ever seen. Jr. followed right behind her, bow and arrow ready. Aiden and Rina both peeked around the corner to watch the fight. They saw Grape running at full speed towards the group, who now were alert.

The soldiers charged back at her, the archers tried to get prepared, only to fall one by one, Jr.'s arrows hitting them before they could return fire. As the archers fell, Grape and the soldiers clashed. She ducked the first soldier, tapping him in the back, sending him stumbling in Jr.'s direction, who quickly fired an arrow, taking down his target.

Aiden quickly learned what their tactics for the soldiers were. Grape was the distraction, soon as Jr. had his shot, he fired his arrows. Each arrow landing in a weak spot in the soldier's armor, each arrow taking down an enemy. The next soldier was more cautious than the first, stopping to meet Grape head on, slashing his sword at her, only to be countered each time. The other soldiers raised their shields and attempted to get closer to the Kaiine.

Grape closed the distance with her opponent, grabbing him by his armor, throwing him towards his comrades, causing them to stumble over each other. The first one to get back to his feet was met with an arrow through his helmet, sending him back down to the cobblestone street. Grape came up behind the next soldier, who raised his shield to block Jr's arrows, only to leave his back open to her daggers sliding under his armor.

The last two soldiers got to their feet with their backs together, shields raised, waiting for the next attack. Grape and Jr. circled the last two soldiers, both on opposite sides of their enemies. Grape made the first move, charging the two soldiers, feigning her attack, forcing her opponent to raise his shield, blocking his line of sight on her. She sidestepped the soldier and attacked the one facing Jr., sinking her daggers in the man's shoulders, both falling to the ground, leaving the last soldier alone, his back open for Jr. to fire his arrow that hit its mark, piercing through the man's neck.

"Let's go!" Jr. shouted to the children.

The group ran out of Cosan, reaching the cover of the forest shortly after the sun started to rise. Soon as they reached the tree line, Jr. turned to watch their backs. Grape and Jr. understood the plan, Grape was to continue with the children while he waited to make sure they were not being followed.

Aiden ran behind Grape, understanding what the strategy was, Rina followed her brother, tears rolling down her cheeks. She did not want to leave anyone behind and felt like she was losing everyone all over again. Ellie ran right beside her, guarding her from any unknown enemies in the woods. Grape led them at a furious pace, trying to stay as far ahead of the Kaskian soldiers as possible.

"I... I can't..." Rina stuttered as she tried to push on, falling to her knees, gasping for air.

Ellie barked, catching Grapes attention as both Aiden and Rina tried to catch their breath. Grape looked around their surroundings, making sure that there was no one following them. She could tell that she was pushing them too hard. "We'll rest here for a few minutes." She told them, handing them both a canteen from the sack that Squishy had given her. "Drink up, and don't forget to give some to Ellie."

Aiden and Rina sat there on the ground, guzzling water as they rested. Ellie drank what she needed and stood guard behind them, her fur standing on edge. Grape stood on the other side of them, daggers in her paws, ready for a fight.

"We need to get moving." Grape said sadly, wanting to give them more time to rest.

"Can we wait a couple more minutes?" Rina asked, not having the energy to go on.

Before Grape could answer, Ellie barked, catching the group's attention. Grape readied her daggers, Aiden pulled his sword from its sheath and both stared in the direction that Ellie was facing. The group waited and listened only to hear nothing. Aiden looked down at Ellie to ask her what it was, only to see her laying on the ground as if there was nothing out there.

"What's wrong Ellie?" Aiden asked, finally hearing a rustling noise coming from the woods.

"It's me!" Jr. alerted the group, not wanting to be attacked by them.

"Jr.!" Rina cheered, running up to him and giving him a hug.

"How did you know?" Grape asked, staring at Ellie.

"She must have picked up my scent. It's how I followed you. I picked up her scent. It's a lot easier to follow than any of yours." Jr. replied. "Are you ready to keep going? It's getting close to mid-day already."

"Was anyone following us?" Aiden asked.

"No. From what I can tell, that squad was alone. When anyone finds them, we were long gone." Jr. answered.

"Then we can travel at a slower pace." Grape stated. "But we need to get moving."

"Do you think Squishy and Arlington are ok?" Rina asked Grape as they walked, eyes brimming with tears.

"Yes, they will be fine." Grape assured her. "They have the advantage. They knew the enemy was there and could set up an ambush."

"Arlington is a lot tougher than he seems." Jr. added.

"How far is the desert from here?" Aiden asked, changing the subject, wanting more information about the journey.

"We should be close by nightfall." Jr. replied, looking up through the trees, trying to gauge where the sun rested. "We will have to find a place to stay before then."

The group pressed on, Aiden listened as Rina attacked Grape with question after question. She asked about where Grape came from, to which she was told that all of them, Squishy, Arlington, Jr., and herself were born in Kaskia. She's never been outside of the country. The questions helped to distract Aiden's mind and pass the time. Before he knew it, the light from the sun started to fade and the forest slowly grew darker.

"Wait." Jr. said, as he ran further ahead of the group, stopping behind the last tree before a clearing.

"What is that?" Rina asked, squinting, trying to make out the structure that she saw in the distance.

"Hopefully where we'll be staying tonight." Grape replied when Jr. gave the signal for them to join him.

"It's an old fort." Jr. told them. "It should be abandoned now, hopefully, but you never know."

Sighing, Grape thought of their next move. Either they check out the fort or keep going and hope to find something a little less risky. "Let's go check it out." She told them.

"Wait, us too?" Rina asked.

"Yep." Jr. answered. "It's not safe for one of us to go check it out, and it's not safe for you three to stay here if both of us go. Only option is for all of us or we keep going."

"Stay alert." Grape told the group as they walked slowly towards the small fort.

Grape held her daggers ready, Jr. had his bow out and arrows prepared, Aiden tightly gripped his sword, and Rina watched in awe. She had always wanted to see a fort. When she was younger, her family would play in a make-believe fort by the lake. Ever since, she has wanted to see what a real one would look like.

As they approached the large wooden doors of the fort, Aiden wondered if there were truly no one living within the walls. He saw lanterns resting calmly on the ramparts, leaving the stronghold in darkness. Squinting, he could barely make out signs of cracks in the walls, seeing that the fort was slowly falling apart over time since the day it was built. It looked as if one solid attack would crumble the wall, leaving it open to an invasion. Just as they reached the doors, they swung open, a loud creak echoing through the night, revealing a dozen men and women armed with swords, clubs, maces, and spears.

"Who are you?" The woman in charge demanded.

"We're just looking for a place to stay for the night." Grape replied, her grip tightening on her daggers.

The woman stared at the group, surprised to see a Bermion, Kaiine, and two children. "It will cost you." She replied.

"How much?" Grape asked.

"They're not going to let us stay here." Jr. whispered to Grape. "They're bandits and stalling before they attack."

"Up there!" Rina yelled as she saw men with bows on the walls.

"Get them!" The woman shouted at her bandits, pointing her splintered club in the direction of the intruders.

Grape, Ellie, and Aiden charged at the group of bandits at the doors. Jr. let loose arrows at the archers on the walls while standing in front of Rina to protect her. Aiden ducked a club that was swung at his head as Ellie bit the next bandit's leg, causing the man to scream in agony.

Grape quickly took the opportunity to strike the man while Aiden dispatched the woman who attacked him with the club. The three of them fought in unison, when Grape dodged, Aiden countered the attack. When Aiden back stepped, Ellie pushed the attacker back only to be met by Grape.

Even though the bandits had them out numbered, they were not trained as well as Grape and Aiden. Jr. and Rina were not as lucky. Although Jr. managed to take out most of the archers, he was struck in the shoulder by an arrow, causing his aim to falter. Try as he could, he was unable to hit his targets and protect Rina from their assaults.

"No!" Rina yelled, all her emotions from the past few days coming to a boil. "Stop hurting my friends!" She continued, summoning six fireballs in front of Jr., who stood there in awe of the floating fireballs that seemed to be catching the arrows, destroying them on impact. As soon as the arrows ceased, the archers, too, stared in awe of the fireballs. "You will not hurt them!" Rina yelled, pointing at the nearest archer, sending a fireball directly at the man.

The archer was too stunned to react, her attack landing directly on his chest, sending him flying backwards, screaming in pain as the fire consumed him, until he slammed into a building within the fort. His body fell silently from the structure, landing in the courtyard below. As she had with the first fireball, Rina pointed at the next archer, who learned from the first mistake, and attempted to run. The fireball soared through the air as the archer jumped from the walls, hoping to be hidden within the fort.

Rina had the target in her mind, the fireball flew past the walls and descended after the archer, disappearing from Jr.'s sight. A sound of her target's scream from the other side of the walls was proof her attack hit its mark. One after another, Rina sent the last four fireballs after the remaining archers, who all attempted to flee from her attack, each one failing miserably.

"That was amazing..." Jr. said, turning to see Rina fall backwards from exhaustion.

"What happened!" Aiden yelled as he rushed towards his unconscious sister.

"She used magic to defeat six archers, she over exerted herself." Jr. answered. "She just needs rest.

"Are you okay Jr.?" Grape asked as she picked up Rina.

"Yeah, the arrow didn't go too deep." Jr. replied, rubbing his shoulder where the wound was.

"I'll look at it once we're safely inside." Grape replied, turning to head inside the fort.

"Aiden, help me shut the doors." Jr. said, using his good arm to lean against the large wooden door.

Grape laid Rina gently on a pile of hay that rested near the front doors of the courtyard. The group quietly checked the rest of the fort, making sure that they were alone. A small barracks rested in the center of the stronghold that had a large crack in the side where the archer had struck it.

Once the fort was secured, Rina was placed on a bed within the barracks where Aiden and Ellie watched over her. With the only entrance to the barracks guarded by Jr. and Ellie, Grape was free to watch over the fort from above. Aiden slowly drifted into sleep, slumped on the floor next to the bed that Rina slept on. Her words haunting his dreams. It's all my fault.

Chapter 12

"How is she?" Grape asked, seeing Aiden sitting by Rina's side.

"She's alright." Aiden answered. "She's been tossing all night."

"Has she woken up at all?" Grape asked.

"Briefly. She drank some water then fell back asleep." Aiden replied. "Is it time to go?"

"Soon." Grape answered.

"Can you wake her up? I need to go stretch my legs." Aiden asked, as he got up from his chair and started to walk out of the barracks, not waiting for a reply.

"Yea." Grape answered as Aiden closed the door behind him.

Aiden walked around the fort, looking at all the gear and items that the bandits had stolen, finding weapons among other supplies. The item that caught his eyes was a shield that rested under a bag of junk. Pulling off the bag, Aiden saw that the shield seemed to be the perfect size for him. Lifting it up in one hand, the weight felt right, Aiden pulled out his sword and began to practice with his new gear.

Jabbing his sword at an imaginary opponent then lifting his shield to block the attack of another, then swinging the shield outward to bash the attacker he blocked. Feeling satisfied with the shield, he slung it over his shoulder, leaving it resting on his back.

Aiden then placed the sword back in its sheath then began pacing around the courtyard, testing out how the two items felt while traveling. Aiden continued to practice with the shield and sword, drawing both from their resting places to get comfortable with each, never knowing how fast he would need to draw both.

"Go Aiden!" Rina cheered, breaking Aiden from his testing of the equipment.

"Oh." Aiden replied, satisfied with the shield and sword, placing them where they belonged. "Are we ready to go?"

"Yes." Jr. replied, coming through the front doors of the fort. "We're maybe an hour from the desert. Once we get there, we need to travel about an hour or so into the desert, then continue heading east."

"Jr.!" Rina said excitedly, rushing to give the Kaiine a hug. "How's your arm? You got hurt protecting me."

"It's ok. Don't worry Rina, I'm fine." Jr. replied, patting her on the head. "You're the one who saved me. You got all the archers with one spell, very impressive."

"I did?" Rina asked confusedly, not remembering what had happened.

"Yes, you did, Rina." Grape replied. "We'll tell you about it once we're on our way."

Aiden was the first to leave the fort, Ellie following on his heels, eager to continue their journey. Grape and Rina waited for Jr., who was leaving a note for Arlington and Squishy, letting them know which direction they were heading. Aiden continued to walk in the front of the group, not wanting to chat with anyone, feeling the weight of the situation wearing on him, Rina's words echoing in the back of his mind, reminding him how he had failed.

The sun was rising, as the trees were fading away. The further they traveled south, the fewer trees were in the forest until they finally disappeared altogether, leaving only an open field of grass. In the distance, Aiden could see a glimmer on the horizon. He assumed that was where the desert waited for them.

Rina and Grape trained while they walked, practicing her skills with the daggers. This time, Grape was showing Rina how to throw her daggers and telling her that sometimes during battle, it helps to be able to throw it, but she shouldn't just throw them all the time, because if she does, then she will be unarmed and at a disadvantage.

The closer they got to the desert, the hotter it was getting. Aiden was drenched in sweat just from walking, his new shield becoming far heavier and harder to carry than he initially thought.

"We're going to rest here for a few before we go into the desert." Grape said, finding a lone tree that sprouted from the ground, providing a little shade for the group. "Drink plenty of water, we all have to stay hydrated."

"Why is it so hot." Rina pouted, drinking from the canteen while wiping sweat from her forehead.

"It's just how it is in the desert, and why we are not going too far into it." Jr. replied, taking a sip of water. "Just far enough to stay out of sight."

"Here." Grape said, pulling out some lightweight cloaks from the bag of supplies. "Use these to cover your head. It will help protect your face from the sand and sun." She continued as she handed out a blanket to each of them, helping to place one over Ellie, then pausing as she handed one to Aiden, who hasn't said a word since they left the fort. "Are you ok Aiden?"

Aiden nodded in response, staying quiet as he waited for the group to head into the desert. His mind still reeled from the thoughts that everything was his fault. All Aiden wanted to do was to get to this ally of theirs and find a way to rescue his parents. Grape told the group to take one last drink before they were heading out. Jr. pulled his cloak over his head and started walking ahead of the group. Grape explained that he was scouting again, making sure that it was safe. The desert was an unknown and they were not sure what was out there waiting for them.

They walked for what felt like an eternity in the desert. There was no breeze, just blue sky and a burning sun bearing down on them. Aiden and Rina tried as hard as they could to keep going, their bodies wanting to give up on them with every step they took, their feet sinking into the sand, adding another struggle to their journey. Aiden looked up, covering his eyes with his hand, seeing that the sun was directly above them. He wanted this trip to be over, he was exhausted and wanted to sleep for days.

"Grape!" Jr. yelled, waving to them from a sand hill waiting in the distance.

"It's Jr." Rina said, too exhausted to be excited.

"Hopefully he found something." Grape replied, feeling tired as the heat wore on her.

"There looks to be some sort of temple to the east." Jr. told the group as they made their way to him. "Past that next sand hill." He said, pointing at the sand hill that blocked the horizon.

"Good. We'll rest there." Grape told the group, as she pushed on.

Aiden sighed and marched on behind the group. Wiping the sweat from his forehead, he looked at his surroundings, seeing that there were no signs of life in any direction. The only thing in sight was sand everywhere. He wondered, if Squishy and Arlington were following them, how they would possibly be able to follow them through the desert. They had been trudging through the desert for a few hours, the sanding making the trip take longer than they had expected.

"See? It's over there!" Jr. said at the top of the sand hill, pointing out of sight of everyone who was still trying to make their way up.

"Yay..." Rina cheered weakly.

"Almost there." Grape sighed, exhausted, trying to motivate the others as much as herself. "It looks like there's some shade too."

The group hurried their way towards the temple, a small pyramid with a small building resting to the side of it. Jr. ran ahead of the rest of the group, taking a quick look at the surroundings, making sure there were no surprises for them. The temple was small enough that Jr. managed to jog around the perimeter by the time the group arrived at the small building.

"No one's here from what I can tell." Jr. told them. "I wouldn't go near or in the temple itself. From the size above ground, I believe there's more underground, it would be easy to get lost."

"Understood." Grape acknowledged. "What's in the building?"

"Looks like it was a storage or supply room when whoever built this." Jr. answered, pointing back at the temple. "It should be safe for us to rest. I don't think we should continue on until tomorrow morning, before the sun comes up."

"I agree." Grape said, as she walked into the small building, dropping the sack of supplies. "Drink water and rest."

Rina plopped onto the ground, into a pile of sand that had been blown in from the outside. She drank water from her canteen before falling backwards, laying down in the sand, exhaustion taking over. "Can I take a nap?" She asked, falling asleep before anyone could answer her.

Aiden found a small wooden cup and filled it with water, placing it on the floor. "Here Ellie, drink." Ellie followed Rina's example, drinking water then walking over to where she slept in the sand and laid down next to her. Aiden dropped all his gear on the floor, placing his cloak on his shield, trying to make it feel more comfortable to be used as a pillow, before laying down to rest himself.

"They must be exhausted." Grape said to Jr.

"They're only children and were not raised for this like we were." Jr. replied, as the two watched the kids sleep.

"You should get some rest too." Grape told Jr. "You need to let your wound heal. I'll look around and make sure everything stays quiet."

Jr. and Grape woke to the sound of Ellie growling. "I must have fallen asleep." Grape stated, rubbing her eyes. "What's wrong Ellie?"

Grape and Jr. looked out the door in the direction that Ellie was staring at to see five hooded figures standing there staring back at them as the sun was slowly setting on the horizon. "Wake them up." Grape told Jr. as she stood her ground in the doorway, wishing that she had her daggers on her.

"What's going on?" Rina asked as she got to her feet, still feeling sleepy.

"We're not alone, stay quiet." Jr. told her. "We don't know who or what they are." As he picked up his bow and quiver, then grabbed Grapes daggers from where she had left them.

Aiden picked up his shield and sword, preparing for the possibility of a fight, as Jr. gave Grape her weapons and nocked an arrow, waiting for the signal.

"Who are you and what do you want?" Grape yelled at the hooded figures, who looked at each other confused.

"What are they?" Aiden whispered, amazed at the sight of the newcomers. Who stood over seven feet tall with a long skinny neck. Each one had a cloak that covered their heads and wore leather armor covering only their chests and legs, leaving their arms vulnerable. Their skin made him shiver, they had no hair anywhere that he could see, their skin seeming like scales, almost that of a lizard. That's when Aiden noticed why Grape and Jr. had their weapons ready, each creature had a sword resting on their waist.

"Be ready." Jr. told Aiden and Rina, ignoring the question about the creatures standing before them.

The one who stood in the middle, Aiden assumed was the leader, said something in a language that none of the group could understand, to his comrades. The creature next to the leader leaned close, whispering its response to the superior, before drawing its sword, raising it high in the air and shouting to the others, causing them to unsheathe their swords and charge. Grape, Ellie, and Jr. jumped into action, Grape rushing towards the lizard people while Jr. shot arrow after arrow.

Ellie did her usual routine of distracting her opponents who seemed unsure of her. Aiden and Rina stood stunned at how the creatures moved with such speed rivaling Grape and Jr. Each arrow that the Kaiine sent flying at his enemies was deflected or dodged, he was unable to land any of his shots. Grape pushed on fighting as hard as she could, even while Ellie distracted them, she wasn't able to hit her opponents.

"They're losing." Aiden stated, snapping out of his shock, charging into battle, leaving Rina standing in the doorway alone, terrified of the creatures. Her thoughts returned to her dreams, the army in the darkness, wondering if this was what her nightmares were warning her about. Creatures that were far too powerful to face, creatures that made her body tremble in fear.

Jr. slung his bow on his back and began fighting the lizard people with his paws. With Ellies help, he managed to get a sword away from one of the creatures and fought another ferociously as the one went to retrieve his weapon. Grape was surrounded, fighting off two as the third went around to sneak up on her from behind, swinging its sword in a downward arc, an attack that would split her in two.

Aiden ran as fast as he could to her, dropping his sword to hold his shield up with both hands, preparing mentally to block the incoming attack. Eyes wide, Aiden struggled to hold off the sword as it struck his shield, full weight of the attacker slamming down into his defense, making Aiden fall to one knee as he tried with all his might to hold back the strike.

The lizard used its weight and strength to push the sword down, forcing the shield to slowly fall to his chest. Aiden's arms trembled under so much pressure, feeling the tip of the blade slice into his shoulder. Screaming in agony, fighting with all his might to hold the shield from dropping completely.

Try as she could, Grape could not get the two off of her to help Aiden, Jr. too, watched in horror as he tried to push his attacker away, and failed as Grape did, barely being able to fend off its attacks. Ellie barked as she tried to come to Aiden's side, only to be grabbed, by the creature who lost his weapon, and thrown in the opposite direction.

Aiden's scream broke Rina out of her freight. As she had done before, she summoned her magic, bringing to life a fireball in front of her, a fireball far larger than any she had previously made, rivaling the size of Ellie. Rina cast the ball of fire towards the lizard attacking her brother, landing it directly into the side of the creature, sending it flying across the sand. The remaining lizards were distracted by the power she wielded, giving Jr., Grape, and Ellie the chance to push off their attackers and to get Aiden to safety. As they retreated towards the building, the lizard that Rina hit stood up from the sand, dusting itself off.

"How could it get up from that?" Jr. said, pulling his bow back out with an arrow, trying to figure a way out.

"Rina, can you do that again?" Grape asked. "If you can distract them, then we could run. We cannot defeat them."

"I... I will try." Rina said, trying to muster the strength of will to face these beings that terrified her.

The five lizard people regrouped and prepared to charge again. Swords in their hands, the leader gave that same order as before, causing the creatures to renew their assault. Rina summoned her fireballs again, this time with less power and sent them flying at their enemies. Jr. knew that they would dodge the fireballs, for when they did, he fired arrows where they would be, managing to hit two of the lizard people who still pushed forward. "Grape!" Jr. yelled as she was placing Aiden on the inside the building.

Just as Grape came out to help defend the children, an arrow came from the desert to hit one of the creatures neck, causing it to fall to the ground stumbling and forcing the remaining lizard people to slow their assault which was met by a figure jumping from the roof of the building, shield extended, slamming into two of the attackers. Realizing that Squishy and Arlington had finally caught up to them, Grape and Jr. renewed their assault. With the full group there, the lizard people acknowledged that they were now overpowered, and retreated, picking up their wounded comrade who still had an arrow sticking out of its neck, and fled into the desert.

"Perfect timing!" Grape said, giving Squishy and Arlington hugs.

"Aiden!" Rina cried, as she sat next to her wounded brother, who was clutching his shoulder with a deep gash in it.

Forgetting about their reunion, the group rushed inside to Aiden, Squishy asking to see the wound. "Aiden. I can help, but it's going to hurt." Squishy told him.

"Do it...." Aiden grunted in agonizing pain.

"Rina. I need your help." Squishy said, grabbing what little wood was in the room into a pile. "Please light these."

Wanting to help her brother, Rina did as he said, summoning a small flame to ignite the pile. She watched as Squishy took one of Grapes daggers and held it over the flame, turning it over to get both sides of it searing red hot. "What are you doing?" She asked, tears running down her face.

"I'm going to seal the wound, so he stops bleeding and keep it from damaging his arm." Squishy said, handing Aiden a cloak. "Bite on this. Grape, Jr., hold him still." He continued, holding Aiden's neck still as he slowly pressed the burning dagger over the wound, causing Aiden to scream louder than when he had received the wound. Rina wept as she saw her brother suffering, wishing she could do something to take away his pain, Ellie barked anxiously, not knowing what to do. By the time Squishy removed the dagger, Aiden passed out from pain.

"He will be fine." Squishy told Ellie and Rina, as he cut a cloak into a bandage, wrapping the wound. "He needs rest though."

Rina and Ellie rushed to him, Rina crying uncontrollably as Ellie licked his face. Squishy, Grape, and Jr. walked outside the building, leaving Arlington with the kids as they discussed what had happened.

"Do you know what they were?" Grape asked Squishy about their attackers.

"I'm not sure, but I think I read something about them in a book." Squishy said, trying to remember what he read during his studies. "If they're what I think they are, we're lucky that there were only five."

"We wouldn't have survived if you two didn't show up." Jr. added.

"We'll have to stay alert tonight, we can't go anywhere until Aiden is able to travel." Grape stated. "Please tell me that the soldiers are not following us here."

"No. But there's bad news." Squishy replied. "Kerd was there. He's the one who captured their father, who was taken to the capital to meet Cladon."

"What would he want with their father?" Jr. asked, curious as to why the King himself would want to see anyone.

"Because their father is Erik, the great Anvil Warrior of the Third War." Squishy stated, knowing that both Grape and Jr. had heard the stories of him. How Erik was a fierce fighter and blacksmith that made the weapons for Cladon's army.

"Then that means..." Grape added. "Their mother is Brittany? The Wicked Archer?"

"Yes." Squishy acknowledged. "We have to save them."

"No one has heard from them since they disappeared almost fourteen years ago..." Grape said, realizing that it was because they were pregnant with Aiden. "No wonder he's so skilled at fighting for growing up in the woods." She said in awe.

"That's why they were so hard for the soldiers to defeat." Jr. stated, trying to grasp the situation.

"That's not all." Squishy added. "She was taken to Prison City. Cladon wants her locked up for desertion."

"He's waking up!" Arlington yelled from the doorway of the building.

"We'll talk more about this later. But this changes everything." Squishy said as the trio headed back inside.

"What... What happened?" Aiden asked, rubbing his head with his good hand.

"You blacked out." Arlington said.

"I'm so sorry Aiden!" Rina cried. "It's all my fault!"

"It's not your fault." Aiden said, hugging Rina with one arm. "Are we safe?"

"For now." Jr. answered.

"What now?" Aiden asked, trying to get to his feet, wincing as his shoulder sent pain through his body.

"You rest." Squishy said. "We'll head out tomorrow."

Rina walked over to a corner of the room, crying as she felt horrible that her brother was in so much pain and yet he still wants to continue, when she was so easily frightened by the creatures that attacked them. Ellie followed Rina to the corner of the room, trying to calm her as Rina leaned against the wall and slid to the ground, hearing a loud noise that caught the attention of everyone in the room.

"What was tha..." Rina started to ask as the floor beneath her and Ellie gave way, dropping both into darkness before the floor went back into its natural position, leaving the group stunned.

Chapter 13

"Rina!" Aiden yelled as he watched his sister vanish from sight. Ignoring excruciating pain, he frantically ran to the corner of the room where she disappeared. "What happened to her?!"

"It must be a secret entrance to the temple." Jr. said, crouching in the corner, running his fingers across the wall, feeling for anything that could have opened the trap door.

As soon as Jr. said the word temple, Aiden bolted out of the building, heading for the entrance of the pyramid. Ignoring all protest from the group, he held his wound and ran, pushing his body past its limits, fighting the pain surging throughout his body.

"Jr., Grape, stay here and try to open that door." Squishy stated, picking up a piece of wood that was still on fire. "Arlington, come with me. We have to catch up to Aiden."

Aiden ran through the darkness of the desert, struggling to keep his balance as his feet sunk into the sand with each step. He headed for the opening to the temple, hearing Squishy and Arlington calling for him to wait for them. As he reached the entrance, Aiden knew he wouldn't be able to go any further without some sort of light, the corridor waiting in complete darkness.

"Here." Squishy said, handing Aiden the flaming piece of wood. "See those torches on the wall? Light those. We will find her. Please don't rush, there might be traps inside."

"Oww..." Rina muttered, rubbing her head as she used a wall to get back to her feet. Using the wall to feel her way through the darkness, Rina heard Ellie whimper behind her. "Are you ok Ellie?" She asked, receiving a quiet yip in response. Raising her hand, Rina imagined where it would be within the darkness, picturing a small flame hovering inches above her palm.

Seconds later, a blaze burst into existence, illuminating the hallway where she landed. The corridor was made of sandstone stretching in two directions, both paths waiting in darkness. In front of her, she saw a torch resting on the wall. Pointing her hand towards the tip, Rina focused on transferring the flame from her hand to the torch. Unsure if it would work, Rina watched as the flame floated from her to its new home, igniting the torch on the wall.

"Which way should we go?" Rina asked Ellie as she took the torch from its resting place. She watched as Ellie sniffed the hallway in both directions trying to figure out the best path to take. After a few minutes, Ellie finally barked facing the hallway to her left, indicating her choice.

Ellie and Rina walked cautiously through the temple, following Ellie's nose when picking different corridors to travel through. They found many rooms, sealed shut by heavy wooden doors. Rina assumed they were sealed from the inside or by magic somehow.

After failing to open the first few doors, she ignored all others that they passed. Feeling as if she was in a maze, she wondered if they would ever make it out. The only thing keeping her from going in circles, was lighting all the torches she passed, illuminating the trail behind her.

She felt like the temple went on forever, passing dozens of sealed doors until she finally saw one open at the end of the hallway. The room seemed to glitter from the torch she carried. Rina ran towards the glimmering room, hoping that it was the way out, only to be disappointed by finding a room full of treasure.

Rina stood at the entrance to the treasure room, jaw dropped, staring at all the gold, gems, and trinkets that littered the room. Lifting the torch higher, Rina began walking around the room, taking in all the items, Ellie walking close to her, hair on edge. Rina's attention was drawn towards a wooden desk sitting in the far corner of the room.

A desk that didn't seem to belong in a room full of glorious treasure. The desk was void of any treasure or items except a single scroll resting neatly at the center. Picking up the scroll, Rina saw a green symbol, a green circle with eight triangles evenly distributed around the circle as a seal to the scroll.

Curious to see the contents, Rina broke the seal and unraveled the parchment. She stared at writing in a language she could not read, writing that began to glow before fading off the page. She stared at the scroll confused, turning it over to see the other side. She screamed as the paper burst into flames, sending her flying backwards into a pile of gold coins.

"Rina!" Aiden yelled as they searched the temple. Squishy and Arlington yelled with him, all three of them pausing after each time, listening, waiting, hoping to hear a response from his sister, that or a bark from Ellie. The group quickly found a staircase that led them downwards, in the direction they knew she must be.

They walked and walked, yelling and waiting for a response. Arlington and Squishy both had picked up torches from the walls and carried them on their way deeper into the temple, lighting any torch they passed to help find their way out. Anytime they were forced to backtrack and take a different path, Arlington would use his claws to scratch the wall, indicating that they did not need to go that way when they returned.

"I see light!" Aiden exclaimed, pointing down the corridor, hoping that it was coming from Rina.

"Slow down!" Squishy yelled, trying to catch up to Aiden. "Don't rush!"

The trio reached a four-way intersection in the temple, seeing light going in two directions, leaving one hallway in complete darkness. "One way is where she came from and one is where she went." Arlington stated. "You two go that way, I'll check this way. I'll find my way back if I don't find anything."

"Be careful." Squishy replied as they split up.

Squishy and Aiden continued to walk in the endless maze, calling to Rina, only to hear nothing in return. They passed door after door, all of which Squishy said were probably resting places for the dead. The two attempted to open a couple doors only to fail as all of them were sealed tight. They pushed forward, ignoring the doors and followed the trail of torches lighting their path. Aiden leaned on the wall for support as he stumbled through the corridors. His wound took its toll on him, his body trembling in pain, drenched him in sweat, as he continued to press through the agony. Out of the silence, Rina's scream echoed the temple.

"Rina!" Aiden yelled, running in the direction he thought she was, ignoring the protest from his body, hearing Ellie barking, reassuring him that he was headed in the right path. Moments later, Aiden and Squishy ran into the treasure room, disregarding everything, heading straight to Rina and Ellie, seeing Rina unconscious on a pile of gold coins. "What happened to her?"

"I'm not sure. She's breathing and seems to be ok." Squishy said, looking around the room to see what could have happened, stopping when he saw an old wooden desk resting in a corner with a single scroll perfectly centered on it. Squishy walked towards the desk but was cut off by Ellie who ran between him and the desk, growling furiously at the desk. "I know, Ellie. I'll be okay." Squishy reassured her.

He looked at the scroll, analyzing it without touching it. Looking at it from the side, Squishy saw that there was a seal on the side touching the desk. Squishy grabbed a gold coin that was nearby, and used it to nudge the scroll, rolling it over onto the other side, revealing the seal, gasping as he saw the symbol on the parchment, then looking back at Rina. Squishy quickly pulled out a pouch and nudged the scroll into the bag without touching it. "We have to hurry out of here."

"What is it?" Aiden asked, worried about Rina, unable to assist her with his wounded shoulder.

"I'll tell you when we're out of here." Squishy replied, picking up Rina carefully before guiding Aiden and Ellie back out.

As Squishy, Aiden, and Ellie ran back through the corridors towards the exit, they ran into Arlington who was running in their direction. Squishy quickly told him that they had to leave. The group ran as fast as they could, quickly reaching the steps that led them back to ground level where the exit, Grape, and Jr. waited for them.

"Is she ok?" Grape asked, taking Rina from Squishy. "I'll take her back inside."

"No!" Squishy replied. "We can't stay in that building. We can't risk anyone else falling into a trap and into the temple!"

"What's going on?!" Aiden demanded.

"The temple, those Lizards people. They're connected." Squishy answered. "I couldn't place it until I saw the symbol on this." He continued, opening the pouch so the other could see the green circle with the eight triangles evenly spread around it.

"What is that?" Aiden asked.

"It's the royal seal of Iguania." Squishy answered. "From what I read in my studies, they were just rumors. The only thing that was ever found was this symbol on some old books."

"What books?" Grape asked, also curious as to why she never knew about Iguania.

"From what I could tell, they were history books from Iguania, dating thousands, maybe even tens of thousands of years ago." Squishy replied. "They depict a war with a jungle empire with creatures that resemble Felien."

"I thought Cladon created the Felien?" Jr. asked.

"We all did." Squishy admitted. "These books were rumored to be some sort of story, nothing more than that. I'm beginning to think otherwise. Iguanians were written as extremely powerful and were able to wield devastating magic."

"Then those five were guardians of this temple?" Grape asked.

"I think so." Squishy replied. "Which means there could be more than just those five. We need to be careful and leave early, before sunrise. For now, we will go rest behind the temple and keep watch for them returning."

"What is that?" Arlington asked, staring at Rina's shirt that was glowing by her collarbone.

"That's her necklace." Aiden said as Grape pulled out the necklace from under Rina's shirt.

"Where did she get this?" Grape asked.

"We found it in the abandoned shack that I showed you." Aiden told them. "Why is it glowing?"

"I think it's a trinket." Grape replied. "From what it sounds like, this necklace stole Rina's magic to protect her from the scroll, draining her completely."

"She'll be okay, right?" Aiden asked, scared of what may happen to Rina.

"She should be fine." Squishy added. "Just like you, she needs rest."

Sighing, Aiden sat with Rina while the rest of the group quickly collected their gear and supplies from the building and took them to the other side of the temple. Aiden watched as the moon rose in the night sky, illuminating the desert in a soft glow.

Taking a deep breath, he felt a cool breeze caress his face, as he tried his best to get comfortable, his wound agonizing him with every movement. Ellie stood guard at the center of the camp, where Squishy placed Rina on his cloak, staying alert for any signs of trouble. Aiden winced as the night's chill irritated his injury, sending a sharp pain through his body.

Thoughts crossed his mind, wondering if he would ever be able to fight again. He thought that he may be useless to the group now, which meant useless in helping to rescue his parents. Aiden lay on his back, staring at the night sky, slowly drifting into slumber, sleep tugging at him, pleading for him to close his eyes.

Chapter 14

"Aiden!" Rina yelled, waking from a nightmare drenched in sweat.

"Huh?" Aiden replied groggily.

"Rina? You're awake!"

"What... What happened?" Rina asked, rubbing her head. "My head hurts so much."

"I'm glad you're alright." Aiden replied, hugging his sister with his one good arm.

"Your necklace." Squishy said, pointing to the gem resting in the middle. "It has magic abilities, it must have been enchanted years ago. When it sensed a magical attack on you, it used your magic to defend against it, draining your energy in the process."

"What does that mean?" Rina asked, still confused at what he told her.

"The scroll you opened, it is also enchanted." Squishy replied, showing Rina the scroll in his pouch. "Anyone who opens it is meant to die. It's quite amazing that you had so much power within you that the trinket was able to protect you."

"Really?" Rina asked, holding her necklace up, staring at the shining gem. "This little thing saved me?"

"Yes. It's a good thing you have it." Grape answered. "When we get we're we are going, he should be able to show you how to use that trinket, so you don't pass out every time it protects you."

"Can you tell us who it is we're going to yet?" Aiden asked, curious to know who the mysterious person is.

"Not yet." Squishy replied. "We should be there in two to three days though."

"Where's Arlington and Jr.?" Rina asked, looking around the camp and not seeing the two Kaiine.

"It's early, they're off scouting the rest of the way." Grape answered. "It's better if we get moving now before the sun comes up. It's far cooler when it's dark out."

"If we are where I think we are, we are only a few hours away from ruins just south of the forest. That is our next camp for today." Squishy added. "Once we get there, it's only about a day's journey to our destination."

"Then let's go." Aiden said, eager to be done with the desert, as he tried to pick up his gear, dropping it as pain surged through his body from his wound.

"I'll carry your shield." Grape said, placing it on her back. "Just hang onto your sword."

Sighing, Aiden nodded, too tired and worn out to argue. He hated being unable to carry his gear, feeling like a burden to the group. "Where did you get your shield Squishy?"

"I took it from one of the soldiers." Squishy replied as if it was nothing. "It seemed too big for the man and a good fit for me. Figured I'd take it just in case."

At the thought of seeing Squishy, a giant bear, casually taking an oversized shield from a soldier who was too small to carry it, Aiden burst out laughing, unable to resist the silly image his head pictured.

"What's so funny?" Rina asked.

"Just picturing how Squishy ended up with the shield." Aiden replied. "The situation we're in, it's crazy."

"What do you mean?" Rina asked, confused why her brother was acting the way he was.

"Never mind." Aiden answered, walking away from the temple "Let's go."

"He's feeling overwhelmed." Grape whispered to Rina. "He's been through a lot the past few days and he's exhausted, he just needs a lot of rest."

Squishy caught up with Aiden as they traveled across the desert in the dark of night, a cool breeze filled the air. Squishy wanted to make sure Aiden was alright and not suffering from any side effects from his wound.

He gauged Aiden on how he walked and talked, asking Aiden about his family, where he lived, how he grew up, trying to figure out if he knew about their parent's past. Everything Aiden told him brought Squishy to the conclusion that their parents wanted to stay hidden away from the gaze of Cladon, which meant keeping their past from their children.

Grape and Rina traveled together, Ellie at Rina's side as she always was. The female Bermion continued Rina's training, explaining to her about the different ways to fight against different opponents. That if she was to come against an opponent like Squishy with a hammer, she would be better off keeping her distance.

Grape told her that the daggers are no defense against weapons such as those, that she would have to watch her surroundings and try to catch her opponent off guard and make her attacks count. She also explained that when facing multiple enemies, she must be aware of where they are and their weapons always.

Squishy followed Grapes tactics with training as they walked. He started talking to Aiden about battle tactics and fighting scenarios and what to do when certain situations would occur. Squishy was amazed at the knowledge that Aiden already possessed on the topic. Everything he asked Aiden, Aiden already knew the correct answer on how to react.

Squishy then went into tactics when dealing with armies, giving him scenarios about strengths and weaknesses of two opposing sides, asking what he would do with his army if he was in charge of the situation over a certain battlefield. Again, Squishy was astonished by the response, Aiden was well trained by his father and potentially was a better strategist then Squishy thought of himself. He knew that once his arm was healed, and he got more training, Aiden would become a warrior of legend, surpassing his father.

"It's Arlington!" Rina cheered, seeing the Kaiine that she's grown to care about and considered as someone close to her.

"Hi Rina!" Arlington replied with the same amount of enthusiasm as she had.

"Are we close?" Squishy asked as Arlington joined the group.

"Yep!" Arlington replied, pointing Northeast where the moon faded over the horizon. "We should be there soon. Jr. is already there."

"Why are we staying in ruins?" Aiden asked.

"We have a small hideout there." Arlington answered. "It's hidden under the ruins and keeps us safe when we're in the area and need a place to stay."

"That's so cool!" Rina replied excitedly. "I want to see!"

"We will be there shortly." Grape told her.

The group continued trekking across the desert as the sun rose behind them. The closer they got to the ruins, the more the Kaskian forest began appearing on the horizon. Aiden and Squishy walked in silence, both having a million things on their minds. Grape, Rina, and Arlington talked about their lives, laughing at things they have done or pranks that Arlington had played on Jr. in their travels. Rina told them how she would mess with Aiden when they would go off playing in the woods.

"Is that it?" Aiden asked, pointing at what looked like giant stone pillars, some of which were knocked down, laying on the sand in pieces.

"Yep!" Arlington replied. "After that, it won't take but maybe an hour to reach the forest again. You thought the woods where you lived were dense, wait till you see this side of the country!"

As they approached the ruins, the group saw Jr. waiting on top of one of the pillars. Soon as they neared him, Jr. jumped off the pillar, landing in the sand next to them, signaling for the group to follow him to where the secret entrance to the hideout was. The group followed Jr. towards the center of the ruins where a dozen pillars lay on top of each other, all broken and damaged. Jr. led them to a small gap between two pillars, barely enough space for Squishy to fit into.

The gap led to a small opening that the whole group would never be able to fit in and Aiden shared his thoughts about the hideout. Jr. explained that this was only the front door before sliding a stone slab aside, revealing a ladder that led below the ruins and into a large, furnished, chamber. Aiden saw enough beds that looked extremely comfy, for the entire group, even Ellie, to have her own.

"Make yourselves at home." Squishy stated as he closed the entrance to the hideout. "There's plenty of food here too."

"How are the torches lit already?" Rina asked, staring at torches resting on the walls of the room.

"The room is enchanted." Arlington replied, hopping onto one of the beds. "They never go out unless someone puts them out."

"Aiden." Squishy said. "Let me see your wound. I need to make sure it's not getting infected. Grape, get some bandages and ointment to put on it."

Aiden walked over to Squishy, taking in the image of the room as he struggled to take off his shirt. Squishy took the make-shift bandage off, revealing his wound that had pus and blood leaking out of it. Rina's eyes teared up when she saw the cut in his shoulder, blaming herself for not reacting faster when he was attacked.

"Tell me about Cladon." Aiden told Squishy as he flinched when Squishy applied an ointment that Grape brought him. "I need a distraction..."

"Okay." Squishy replied, gently patting the wound with a cloth, cleaning the area. "A little over three hundred years ago, Kaskia was a part of Premus, a prospering human empire. Everything seemed to be good in the land. There were no wars, no fighting, nothing. Premus has been around for thousands of years without any fighting."

"But then came Cladon. No one knows where he is from or how old he really is. Back then, he was a skilled wizard." Squishy continued as he wiped the wound with another piece of cloth, trying to stop the little bleeding that was there. "We think he started in Toogal, a city to the north. He somehow founded a rebellion in the area, banishing all Premus soldiers from the city, any that he didn't convert to his side."

"This went on for almost ten years. Many lives were lost. Trench, the King of Premus at the time, had had enough of the war. He cared for his people and didn't want to lose any more lives." Grape added as Squishy placed a new bandage on the wound.

"As she said, ten years at war with Cladon and his rebellion." Squishy confirmed. "Trench and Cladon agreed to a treaty, giving Cladon the land he wanted, which was Toogal and where the capital of Kaskia is today."

"Fifty years went by, Kaskia and Premus stayed true to the treaty. But something happened in that time that changed Cladon to become something even worse than what he was." Squishy said, shaking his head. "He must have done something truly horrible to become as powerful as he is, and for what we know, immortal."

"Is that when the second war happened?" Aiden asked, remembering what his parents told him.

"Yes." Grape answered.

"Fifty years of peace ended by Cladon's madness. This time, Cladon had a larger and better trained army. This time, he had the Felien on his side." Squishy stated, sighing when he uttered the word Felien. "The Felien enabled Cladon's army to push Premus back to the Dealay river, just past where you were raised. The only way across the river being a single bridge, it kept both sides from pushing past the river. This war did not last nearly as long as the first. Trench and Cladon came to another agreement and declared that the river was the border between Empires."

"The world lived in peace for well over two hundred years after that, being that both sides had heavy casualties for such a short war." Squishy sighed. "But yet again, Cladon's madness took over. We think that peace only lasted because he didn't have the Felien numbers in his ranks anymore. We're still not sure where he got them, whether he created them or summoned them."

"There was an attack on Osion that Cladon used as a motive to start another war." Grape added. "This is when your parents were in the war."

"Cladon took anyone who was able to hold a weapon." Squishy continued. "Premus never saw it coming. Cladon managed to secure the other side of the bridge and invaded Premus. They lost many lives, Cladon's army managed to push all the way to the capital of Premus and invade the throne. But just as it had started, the war ended. Loson the third, current King of Premus, came to terms with Cladon, even though they denied any attack on Osion."

"Somehow Cladon managed to get Loson to give him an outpost on the other side of the bridge. Giving him the power to invade any time he wants to." Grape added, shaking her head in confusion. "The war doesn't make sense. We think it was all a distraction and that Premus had something of value that Cladon wanted and once he got it, he withdrew his army."

"What did he want?" Aiden asked.

"We don't know." Jr. replied. "That's why we were raised for this. A battle is coming, Cladon is plotting something. Premus has proven time and time again that they will bow to Cladon's demands. Someone needs to stand against him."

"That's us?" Rina asked.

"Yes." Squishy answered. "If you're willing to join us, after we rescue your parents. You both will be strong allies in the upcoming fight."

"That's a lot to think about." Aiden replied. "What do you think Rina?"

"I don't know." Rina admitted.

"You have plenty of time to think about it, you can even wait until we rescue your parents." Squishy added. "For now, eat some food and relax."

The group sat on the beds as they ate a meal of bread, cheese, and deer jerky that was stocked in the hideout. Arlington told stories of where they grew up and their training, how they will love where they're going and how much fun it is there. They spent the day talking about the world and the adventures they all have been on and want to see. Aiden was the first to fall asleep, his injury taking its toll on his body, Rina and Ellie falling asleep not long after.

Jr. and Squishy checked outside, making sure they were not followed from the temple by Iguanians or Kaskian soldiers. The moon high in the night sky, the duo headed back in, joining the others and resting for the night.

Chapter 15

"Aiden, Rina." Grape said, shaking both gently. "It's time to wake up."

The two children slowly got out of bed and began gathering their supplies that they had gathered over the trip so far. Rina with her daggers, cloak, and a small bag of food that she was given the night before. Aiden grabbed his sword, his cloak, and looked for his shield only to be told that Jr. and Arlington had already gone ahead of them, taking his shield and some of the extra supplies with them. Ellie trotted around the room, anxious to be done with the journey.

Squishy, Grape, Aiden, and Rina traveled across the last part of the desert, seeing an open field in the distance and towering pine trees that waited for them on the horizon. The group walked in silence as the sun rose behind them, lighting the path ahead. The closer they got to the trees, the colder the air became.

Squishy explained that beyond the woods were mountains and that it was their destination, and the closer they got to the mountains, the colder the weather would become, that it could potentially snow while they were there. Both Aiden and Rina looked at each other, never witnessing snow for themselves and always wanting to see what it was like. All they knew of it was from the stories their parents told them.

As they entered the woods, Squishy explained that this part of the country had very little civilization, which is why Toogal is such a large city. There were a few people who lived in the woods, but most of the people in the area resided in the city, which was good for them on the last part of their journey.

"Are we going to Toogal?" Rina asked, wanting to see a city.

"No." Grape replied. "Toogal is a very dangerous city. It's no place for you two, especially since you're wanted by Cladon. We are heading up the mountain."

"We should be on the outskirts of Toogal by nightfall." Squishy explained to Aiden and Rina. "When we get near, we will find a place to camp for the night, then we will head for the base of the mountain early tomorrow morning."

"You have a house on the mountain?" Aiden asked, curious how a house could have been built on a mountain.

"Not quite. It's not so much a house. We live in the mountains." Grape answered, confusing Aiden and Rina more than they already were. "You'll understand when we get there." She laughed.

"How do you know which way you're going in these woods?" Aiden asked, amazed that they knew one direction from another, when all he saw were towering trees above them.

"You could navigate the woods around your home, right?" Squishy asked. "It's the same. We grew up out here and memorized the surrounding areas."

The group stopped for a break when the sun was high in the sky. Squishy checked on Aiden's wound, changing the bandage to keep it clean. They ate quietly and drank water, Ellie laying by Rina's side. They were all tired from the journey, lacking the energy to have anything to say. They wanted it to be over. After the small meal, Squishy decided it was best that they kept moving, the sooner they reached the borders of Toogal, the sooner they could rest for the night.

They walked for hours through what seemed like an endless forest to Aiden. His shoulder aching from his wound. Aiden's pace began to slow as he was too drained to keep up with the group, only when Ellie barked at the group did they realize how much he was falling behind. Squishy asked if he wanted to take another break to catch his breath, which Aiden declined, not wanting to be the one who held them from their destination. Rina insisted that he needed to wait, not wanting to see him in pain, tears strolling down her cheeks.

"What are you doing?" Arlington said as he joined the group. "We can't sit still!"

"What's wrong?" Squishy asked. "Where's Jr.?

"Kaskian soldiers are patrolling the woods, they're everywhere!" Arlington explained. "And Jr. already went to head up the mountain to give a report of everything."

"You win, Aiden." Squishy said, feeling the urge to get the group out of the area without being spotted. "We will head east then head to the base tomorrow. We should be safer there."

Arlington left the group again, scouting the area to the east of their current location. Grape led the way as Squishy stayed behind with Aiden, making sure that he did not pass out while they went as fast as he could with his injury. The group went on at that pace for another hour before Aiden was unable to continue. The mountains were in sight and the sun had fallen behind them, leaving the group in the shadow of the peaks.

Squishy dropped his gear and laid his cloak on the ground for Aiden to lay on. Aiden lacked the energy to argue with the Bermion, laying down as instructed. Once he was resting, Squishy told Arlington to go get some firewood to keep them warm. The air was already cold and would only get colder throughout the night.

Grape offered to go with him, helping to accomplish the task faster. Rina sat by Aiden's side, wishing that she could do something to make his pain go away, for she felt that it was her fault he suffered. Ellie lay on his other side, resting her head on Aiden's legs, whimpering softly, as she too felt miserable that one of her family was in so much pain.

As Grape and Arlington returned, Squishy asked Rina to light the logs, giving them warmth for the night while they rested and waited for Aiden to recover enough energy to make the last leg of the trip. As the night went on, Rina stayed next to her brother, both sleeping as Squishy and Grape remained awake, watching over them. Arlington had curled up next to a tree and snored in his sleep as he dreamt the night away.

Aiden tossed and moaned as he slept, nightmares taking over his dreams. He was back home, playing with his sister and Ellie in the woods as they had done thousands of times before. They were by the lake, practicing her magic. Aiden was throwing rock after rock over the lake and Rina was igniting every single one, causing them to burst into rubble over the water.

Next, he threw another rock in a different direction, telling Rina to send a fireball after it. As she had done many times before, Rina summoned a fireball, this time in front of her. Aiden could feel the heat emanating from it as she propelled it forward, racing after the rock.

The fireball caught up to the rock in a matter of seconds, swallowing the rock whole, and kept moving forward, past the lake and into the woods that waited on the other side. As soon as the fireball touched the first tree, it exploded, disintegrating every tree in the immediate area and catching the trees nearest, on fire. Aiden and Rina stood there stunned as they watched the fire spread across the forest on the other side of the lake.

Aiden watched in terror of what they had wrought on the forest when he heard his mother scream. Without a second thought, Aiden rushed back through the woods that rested between him and his house, Rina and Ellie right behind him. As he broke out of the trees, into the clearing where his house waited, Aiden heard another scream from his mother. He ran to the back door, bursting through it and into the kitchen.

Aiden swore his mother was there making dinner, but she was nowhere to be seen. Then he heard her scream again, this time her scream came from the other room. As he had when he heard her last scream, he ran through the door to the next room, again to find it empty, no signs of his mother. He heard her scream for the fourth time, this one coming from outside of the house. Rushing through his home, Aiden burst out of the front doors to see his mother in chains and on her knees with an army of soldiers standing behind her. A single man stood to her side, holding her chains in his gloved hand.

"I have been waiting for you." The man said.

"Who... Who are you?" Aiden asked as he heard Rina scream from behind him. Turning towards his sister, the house had vanished,

Rina now was in chains as his mother was, Ellie locked in a cage next to her. Just as his mother had, an army of soldiers stood behind Rina and Ellie with the forest behind on fire, slowly creeping its way towards them.

"I am your king." Cladon told him.

"You're not my..." Aiden yelled as he turned to face Cladon and his army, stopping as he beheld his mother and sister kneeling in chains with Ellie in a cage next to them. He quickly turned his head behind him only to see the army had him surrounded, the fire ever closer. "You're not my King!" He finished yelling.

"You will bow to me." Cladon demanded of Aiden, snapping his fingers, summoning his father next to him. "Just like your father has bowed, you too, shall bow to me child."

Aiden watched in horror as his father knelt to the mad King. The world on fire around them. "What are you doing?!" He yelled, running to his father's side.

"He is our King." Erik replied, bowing his head as he knelt before the King.

"No!" Aiden cried as he tried to pull his father back to his feet. "He's not our King!"

"Aiden!" He heard Rina call to him, his body shaking with fear as his father shrugged him off and continued to bow to the King.

Aiden turned to look at his sister, who was no longer next to their mother. He heard her call to him again from behind him. Looking behind him, he saw his sister in the house, pounding on the window as she called to him again and again, pleading for him to save her as the fire had taken over their home.

Aiden turned to beg his father to help him save her, only to realize that he was alone. The soldiers, King, and his parents had vanished, only leaving the fire surrounding him. His sister's cry for help gave him focus, ignoring his own safety, Aiden ran for the house, the fire enveloping the world around him.

"Aiden!" Rina yelled again, shaking him, trying to wake him up. "He's not waking up Squishy! What's wrong with him?!"

"He's drenched in sweat." Grape added, worried for Aiden.

"He has a fever." Squishy said, feeling Aiden's forehead. "I think he's hallucinating."

"How do we help him?" Rina pleaded, kneeling next to her brother. "You have to help him!"

"We will." Grape assured her, pulling Rina away from Aiden, holding her tightly in her arms as Rina cried uncontrollably.

"We have to get going!" Squishy stated.

Chapter 16

Squishy slung his hammer over his back and picked up Aiden, as gently as he could, in both arms as Grape put out the fire and gathered all the essential items they needed, leaving everything else behind as they prepared to leave their camp.

Arlington led the group in the darkness of night, followed by Squishy and Aiden, then Grape, Rina, and Ellie bringing up the rear. Arlington told Squishy that they were still, at least, an hour away from the base of the mountain, that they needed to pick up the pace if they wanted to get there sooner for Aiden's sake.

Squishy told Grape to carry Rina as well, since she was the slowest of the group. Rina agreed without any arguments. Grape rested Rina on her shoulders as they picked up their pace to a jog, Ellie keeping alongside Aiden and Squishy as they hurried their way to the mountain.

"We're almost there!" Arlington shouted, seeing the base coming into sight. "There's Jr. too!"

The group picked up their stride, needing to get Aiden to the mountain as soon as possible to heal his wounds.

"What happened?" Jr. asked as the group stopped where he was waiting, catching their breath.

"His wound is infected." Squishy replied, taking deep breaths. "He has a fever and needs to see Teddy right away!"

"Understood!" Jr. replied. "Let me carry him up the rest of the way."

Squishy handed Aiden over to Jr., watching as he took his unconscious body up the mountain, Arlington following behind him. "Don't worry Rina, we'll be right behind them. We just need a minute to catch our breath." Squishy said, taking big mouthfuls of water, then giving some to Ellie.

Grape, Rina, Squishy, and Ellie made their way up the mountain, following the path where Jr. and Arlington ran, they made their way up the trail more cautiously. Jr. and Arlington had far better balance and agility to traverse the mountain faster than Grape or Squishy.

"Where am I?" Aiden muttered to himself, rubbing his head as he looked at his surroundings. He was sitting on a small cot in a stone room that had an iron door with a small square hole towards the top. Aiden got out of the bed and walked to the door, standing on his toes to get a glance of the other side of the door, only to see a hallway with dozens of doors just like his. "Am I in a cell?"

"You are where I want you to be." Cladon stated, staring at him through the door. "You have information that I need, child."

"Where's my family?!" Aiden demanded. "What did you do to them?!"

"You shall see them, soon." Cladon answered. "Only after you give me what I want."

"What do you want then?" Aiden asked, walking away from the door to sit back on the bed.

"The name of the one who used magic." Cladon told him. "And the name of the one you were on your way to meet."

"I don't get it." Aiden muttered. "You have Rina, and I was never told the name of who we were meeting."

"The other child..." Cladon said, scratching his chin. "Interesting."

"Why is it so hot in here..." Aiden asked, as he rubbed his shoulder, wincing in pain. "Why does my shoulder hurt?"

"Come child." Cladon told Aiden, reaching his hand to help him to his feet. "Let's go see your family."

"How did you get in here..." Aiden asked, when he noticed that he was no longer in the cell, he was back home in his room. "What's going on?"

"Aiden!" Rina yelled. "Wake up!"

"But I am awake." Aiden yelled back, running past Cladon, leaving his room behind to run down a staircase that led him into the desert temple. "Rina!"

"Very interesting." Cladon said as he followed Aiden through the maze of corridors, watching as Aiden entered the room where Rina lay unconscious.

"Not again..." Aiden said, seeing Rina lying on the ground next to the wooden desk with the scroll in her hand. "The Iguanian's did this..."

"He needs to see Teddy!" Aiden heard Squishy say.

"Where are you Squishy? Who's Teddy?" Aiden asked.

"Teddy...." Cladon spat as he uttered the name.

"Help Aiden!" Rina cried as they caught up with Jr. and Arlington, seeing them stand over Aiden, who lay motionless on the ground.

"Don't worry Rina." Squishy told her. "Teddy will help him."

Rina stared at Squishy confused, unsure who this Teddy person was. All she saw were Jr. and Arlington bent over Aiden. She gasped when the two Kaiine turned to face them, revealing a third person with them, kneeling over Aiden. There was another Bermion, a much older one, with a paw over Aiden's forehead, a green aura emanating from his hand to Aiden.

Where Squishy had light brown fur, this new Bermion had a darker coat with a gray beard hanging from his muzzle. Teddy glanced in her direction as his aura continued to feed into Aiden. She saw exhaustion in the old Bermion's eyes, not from the use of magic, but from a lifetime of struggle.

"Do not worry." Teddy told her. "He will be okay. Squishy, take him inside to a bed."

Rina watched Squishy pick up Aiden and wondered where they were going. The group stood on a cliff that rested halfway up the mountain. She saw no cave, no doors, no entrance to any sort of home. As if reading her mind, Teddy turned towards the mountain, raising his arms towards the sky. Where before he had a green aura emanating from his paws, this time his body radiated with a blue aura. Rina watched, amazed as a portion of the mountain parted, revealing a hallway behind the rocks.

"He's very powerful." Arlington whispered to Rina.

Squishy rushed through the hallway, taking Aiden out of sight. Teddy escorted the rest of the group into his home. Gesturing to them to put their gear away while he took Rina to where Aiden was going to recover, Ellie stuck to Rina's side the whole time. Rina took in all her surroundings, the old Bermion's home was amazing.

The hallway opened into a large room with cushions to sit on all over, and what she thought was the kitchen area on the opposite side. To their left and right were two more hallways, Teddy guided her to the left. He explained to her that this area was where they tended to their wounded. Sometimes they would get hurt during training, or as her brother had, during a mission.

"He's in here." Teddy reassured Rina as he opened a door, revealing Aiden laying on a bed, Squishy standing next to him, waiting for them.

"Aiden..." Rina said softly, tears strolling down her face. Ellie yipped as she went to the bed, standing on two paws so she could lick his face, trying to wake him up.

"He will be okay Ellie." Squishy said. "Right Teddy?"

"In time, yes." Teddy replied. "He suffered from the wound, which got infected and caused the fever."

"Suffered?" Squishy asked, confused. "His wound is healed already?"

"Yes. The wound is no more." Teddy admitted. "The hallucinations and nightmares were not from the wound. Cladon somehow managed to get into his head."

"What do you mean?" Rina sniffled, scared of what it meant. "Will he be okay or not?"

"He will be fine. But it will take time for him to recover from the mental attack." Teddy replied, placing his hand on Rina's shoulder. "I have to figure out how Cladon managed to enter his mind."

"Come Rina." Squishy said, understanding what Teddy meant. "I'll show you to your room."

"I'm not leaving Aiden!" Rina argued, receiving a bark from Ellie in agreement.

"Teddy needs some time with Aiden to help him get better." Squishy told her. "He will be ok."

"You can come back and see him when I'm done." Teddy added. "I promise, I will help him recover to his old self."

Sighing, Rina reluctantly left Aiden in Teddy's care. Ellie, however, refused to leave Aiden's side, something that Teddy had deemed acceptable. Squishy and Rina walked further down the hallway that led to more rooms, one of which Squishy told her that if she wanted to sleep there, that the room was hers. He also said that she was more than welcome to stay with Aiden once Teddy was done.

Rina looked around her room, which had a bed, a desk, chair, and a candle on the desk. "How long do you think it will be until he's awake?" She asked, as she sat in the chair.

"I don't know, Rina." Squishy replied. "Teddy will do everything he can to help. Once he is done analyzing Aiden, he will have a better answer."

"Hi Rina." Grape said, as she entered the room to join them. "How is he doing?"

"The wound is healed." Squishy answered. "But Cladon managed to get into his head, that's why he's not awake."

"Can Teddy help?" Grape asked.

"He said he can, but it will take time." Squishy replied, as Rina sat in the chair quietly staring at the flame of the candle. "Can you stay with her as I go report to Teddy?"

"Of course!" Grape replied, sitting on the bed next to the desk where Rina sat.

"How is he?" Squishy asked as he entered Aiden's room where Teddy had both hands above Aiden's head, his green aura emanating between the two.

"Stable." Teddy replied. "I'm worried about what Cladon has done inside his head."

"How do you think he managed to reach Aiden?" Squishy asked, concerned that such a feat should have been impossible. Cladon has never met or seen Aiden.

"The only thing I can think of." Teddy sighed. "Their father. If Cladon got into his mind, he could potentially find a link to Aiden. I'm afraid that Cladon has gotten stronger than we thought."

Squishy paced the room, going over their journey from when they rescued the kids near their home. Squishy explained how Rina had used her magic multiple times with power she should not be capable of. He went into detail when he talked about the confrontation of the Iguanians and the temple, opening the pouch to show the scroll to Teddy.

"That's the seal of Iguania alright." Teddy agreed. "You all are very lucky to have survived that encounter."

"What does that mean?" Squishy asked, knowing that Teddy had more information on the Iguanian empire.

"I've never come against them." Teddy admitted. "But from what I've gathered, over the years, is that they are very powerful physically and magically. It sounds like you came across some sort of religious guardians that watch over the crypt."

"If they have magic, why haven't you been able to sense them? Or even Cladon?" Squishy asked.

"They may have magic far more powerful than either of us." Teddy sighed, shaking his head. "And if that's the case. We will have to revisit the situation and investigate more, if we survive Cladon's rule."

"I hope they're not hostile as the guardians were." Squishy stated.

"What else did you learn on your journey?" Teddy asked, pulling a blanket over Aiden's upper body, after he finished with his examination.

"Their parents." Squishy replied, pointing at Aiden. "They're the Anvil Warrior and the Lightning Arrow."

"Very interesting." Teddy replied, scratching at his beard. "The prophecy may be unfolding in front of our eyes."

"You think it's referring to them?" Squishy asked, staring at the unconscious boy.

"The children of Metal and Lightning shall end the reign of darkness, bringing an era of prosperity to the land." Teddy recited. "One shall become King, the other will unite all the realms against the scaled demons."

"You think Metal and Lightning refers to their parents?" Squishy asked, astonished what it would mean if Aiden and Rina were the children of the prophecy.

"Never in my days would I think the two of them would end up together and have two children that fit the prophecy." Teddy admitted, admiring the strength of the boy and the torment he's fighting against. "What worries me is the scaled demons. If this is true, and Cladon is the darkness. The true enemy are those demons."

Teddy questioned Squishy about Aiden and Rina's abilities and what they knew. First, he stated the skill that Aiden had with weapons, that he fought at an advanced level with a dagger, then when he took up the shield and sword, out-skilled himself with it. The only thing that kept him back was the lack of confidence in his fighting and the experience of battle.

Then Squishy explained that Aiden was a tactical genius. Every scenario that Squishy gave him, Aiden found the best answer and even some that Squishy, with all his training, had never seen.

Squishy then talked about Rina and her magic. He explained how she summoned so much fire in the fireplace that the flame went flying out the roof, yet the whole time, she managed to contain it to her target. Squishy told Teddy that her power seems to come from her emotions, that she's strongest when someone she cares about is in danger.

When Aiden got hurt, she summoned a fireball as large as she was and sent it flying into the Iguanian, who somehow managed to come out of the encounter unscathed. But the biggest feat that she accomplished, was surviving the scroll's attack, although she lost consciousness due to the trinket she had, she had enough power inside her to protect her from Iguanian magic.

Teddy paced the room, taking in all the information of the situation. Believing he has the children of prophecy, which put them at an advantage, of sorts. Cladon, on the other hand, has the famed Anvil Warrior and Lightning Arrow, and worst of all, he has been inside Aiden's head.

"If Aiden is truly the child of prophecy." Teddy muttered to himself. "Does Cladon now know? Will Aiden recover and be able to fulfill his destiny?"

"Come in!" Rina answered when she heard a knock on her door.

"Greetings, Rina." Teddy said as he entered the room. "We haven't been properly introduced. I am Teddy, I am a Master Wizard."

At the title of Master Wizard, Rina turned to face the old Bermion. "Is he really?" She asked Grape who still sat next to her.

"Yes, he is." Grape answered.

"Since your brother cannot answer this, it is your choice on what you want to do." Teddy explained. "We know where your mother is, she's in Prison City, a city filled with well-trained Kaskian Soldiers."

"Is she okay?" Rina asked, her eyes brimming with tears.

"From what we know of, yes. She is safe for the moment. I will be sending Jr. and Arlington to keep an eye on her and report back any changes." Teddy continued. "As for your father, all we know is that he is somewhere in the capital, with Cladon. As with your mother, our reports state that he too is alright."

"What... What do I need to do?" Rina asked, tears fully streaming down her cheeks as she felt truly alone. Her mother was in some high security prison while her father was with a mad sorcerer, then there was her brother who had been unconscious for almost a day and showed no signs of waking up anytime soon.

"Do you want to train and become stronger to help free your parents, both of them? Which will be very dangerous." Teddy offered. "Or do you want to wait and let us try to save them. Your brother will get the same choice when he wakes up, however, from what I've been told, I believe he has already made his choice."

Rina sat in silence, wiping tears from her face. Thinking about all that they have been through over the past few days, all that she had been through. The danger she had faced. Many times, she had thought she was done for, yet somehow, they survived everything Cladon sent at them.

She knew that Teddy was right, Aiden had already made his mind up. He would do anything to protect his family and save their parents. She was terrified, she wished above everything else, that she could go back to her life before her parents were taken away and keep living the life she had. Rubbing the last tear out of her eye, filled with determination to be stronger, Rina answered. "I will fight."

Chapter 17

"Rina! Where are you?!" Aiden yelled as he ran through the woods.

"Boo!" Rina shouted back, jumping from behind a tree.

"Ha... ha..." Aiden replied. "That's not..." He paused, feeling as if they had already gone through this.

"Not what?" Rina asked, poking her brother in the arm. "Not what?" She repeated herself, this time her voice deeper, rougher than a girl of her age should be.

"What?" Aiden asked, his head feeling fuzzy.

"Run little human." Rina said, this time in a voice that was not hers.

Aiden stared at his sister as her skin grew scales, her arms, legs, and neck stretching to an inhuman length. Her head altering into that of the lizard people that had attacked them. "What... What's happening to you?!"

"Run boy, run!" The lizard creature ordered, raising a sword into the air.

Scared of what he saw, Aiden turned and ran, running through the woods as fast as he could, hearing the mocking voice of the lizard who was his sister, yet not. Moments later, Aiden burst from the woods, seeing his house in the distance. The faster he ran, the further the house became. Aiden slammed into the door of his room, falling backwards onto the floor.

"How did I end up in my room?" He thought, rubbing his head.

"Are you alright, honey?" Aiden heard his mother ask from the other side of the door. "I heard a loud noise."

"Mom!" Aiden yelled, springing to his feet to open the door of his room.

"Yes dear?" His mother asked.

"Mom..." Aiden stuttered as he beheld the sight of the creature with his mother's voice. Aiden stood there facing the same lizard creature, that now wore the same clothes as his mother, had her voice, her personality, yet was not her.

"What's wrong Aiden?" She asked, reaching a hand towards him. "What's wrong child?" She said, this time in another voice. A voice that Aiden had heard before. The only voice that ever referred to him as a child.

"It's okay Aiden..." Rina whispered to her sleeping brother as he showed signs of having a nightmare. "Everything will be okay."

"He's having another nightmare?" Teddy asked as he stood beside her, placing his hand over Aiden's head. "I will ease his mind. You should go eat some breakfast with the others."

Nodding to Teddy, Rina left Aiden's room to join Squishy, Grape, Jr., and Arlington, who all sat on cushions on the floor, each eating their fill of bread, cheese, and various types of meat. Squishy asked if she would like to try some of his food, which she politely declined, asking for only some bread and any fruit that they may have.

"Rina, don't be afraid, okay?" Grape said, kneeling next to her. "Your brother will wake up and we will rescue both of your parents."

"I'm not afraid anymore." Rina replied, holding her head high. "I will become stronger and save them all!"

"I'm glad to hear that, Rina!" Grape stated, giving her a hug. "We will be back in a few days, try to learn everything you can from Teddy."

"Where are you going?" Rina asked, frowning that Grape, someone who she has come to think of as her best friend, was leaving her.

"I'm going to try and find out where exactly they have your mother, so when the time comes, we can rescue her." Grape answered. "Arlington and Jr. are going to search for your father."

"Please be safe!" Rina said, hugging Grape tightly, then running to Jr. and Arlington and hugging both. Only receiving a genuine hug back from Arlington, Jr. only patting her on the back awkwardly.

"Don't worry Rina, Jr. isn't much for affection." Arlington laughed, making Rina smile. "Take care of Squishy and Teddy while we're gone, Okay? They're lost without us!"

"I will!" Rina said, feeling a little hope creeping into her heart. "Be safe!"

"We will!" Grape replied as the entrance of Teddy's home closed behind them.

"Are you ready to begin?" Teddy asked Rina.

"Yes." She replied.

"Then follow me." Teddy told her as he walked down the hallway opposite of where her brother rested. "Squishy will be watching over Aiden, he will come get us if anything changes."

"What is Ellie doing?" Rina asked, hoping that she was alright.

"She hasn't left Aiden's side. Squishy brought food and water for her." Teddy answered, guiding Rina through the long hallway. "She's worried about Aiden and cares deeply for the two of you."

"She's our family." Rina stated. "What is this place?"

"It's my library, it's where I do my studying." Teddy replied as the two entered a large two-story room, filled with books. "Upstairs is where we're going to start."

Rina looked at all the books, eagerly, wanting to see their contents and what information they held. She followed Teddy towards the center of the room where a spiral staircase waited to take them to the upper floor, where Rina found less books and more open space with a large table in the center.

"I have already placed a book for you to start with." Teddy said. "First, you need to learn the basics of magic before you can use your power to the fullest. So far, you have proven very skilled in what you know you can do. Now, I will show you what you don't know."

Rina hung to every word Teddy told her, hungry to learn everything he had to teach her.

"Can you read?" Teddy asked bluntly, knowing that many in Kaskia were not privileged to that skill, something Cladon used to oppress his people.

"A little." Rina admitted. "Mommy taught me, but we never finished."

"That should be enough, for now." Teddy told her. "Basic reading is enough for us to get started."

"Yay!" Rina cheered, excited that her reading level was good enough.

"I wrote this book years ago." Teddy said, handing her a leather-bound book that she read aloud.

"Con... Con... troll... ing Magic." Rina stuttered.

"Controlling. Good. Read what you can, ask me any questions that you need." Teddy explained as he sat on the floor and began meditating.

Rina sat at the table, reading through the book, pausing to ask questions about how to pronounce certain words and the definition of others. Teddy explained concepts to her as he sat on the floor, legs folded, eyes closed, meditating the whole time she studied. The morning went on in this fashion, only stopping for lunch and to check on Aiden, the latter, still sleeping peacefully.

"Do you have an understanding of the concept?" Teddy asked her as they returned to the library.

"I... I think so." Rina said, trying to think of the right words. "To use magic... I have to do more than just imagine what I want. I have to create the spell in my head, using my mind to create what I picture and bring it into the world?"

"Correct." Teddy said. "So far, you have been casting spells based off instinct and with little control over your energy."

"How do I control my energy?" Rina asked.

"Like this." Teddy replied, focusing on his hand, summoning a small flame that grew larger, changing color from the natural reddish orange hue to a dark blue. As Rina watched, her jaw dropped, Teddy used his other hand summoning a small portal above it that dropped a candle into his paw. "Watch closely." He continued as he turned the hand with the fire upside down, over the candle, lighting it with the blue flame, then placing the candle on the table gently.

"That was awesome!" Rina cheered excitedly. "How did you do that?!"

"Let's start with the flame." Teddy said, extinguishing the candle. "Summon your flame, but only the size of the wick on the candle."

Doing as Teddy instructed, Rina attempted to summon a small flame, failing miserably as she almost burnt down the table the candle rested on. Teddy quickly put the fire out, using his own magic. Rina, determined and reassured by the old Bermion to keep trying, summoned flame after flame, each one slowly becoming smaller and smaller, until she finally lit the wick the way he had done.

"Good, good." Teddy praised Rina, amazed that she was able to summon so much fire and contain it to the size he instructed without tiring, something that had taken him a long time to master in his youth. "Now do it again." He ordered, snapping his finger, extinguishing the small flame she had worked so hard to bring to life.

Rina started to protest, but stopped herself, knowing that in order for her to become stronger, she needed to learn from the Master Wizard, which meant following his instructions. Again, she summoned the flame to the size he had demonstrated, and again, he smothered it with the snap of his finger. The two continued this over and over until Teddy was satisfied that she had mastered the technique.

"Now match the size of the flame that I summon." Teddy told her as he summoned a flame the size of his fist, over his hand.

As she had done with the small flame, she concentrated on summoning another flame that floated above her hand. At first the flame was too small, so she stopped the spell and recast it only to summon one too large. Rina grinned as a thought occurred to her. (Why stop and recast... I should be able to shrink it...) Concentrating hard, imagining the flame the size of his, Rina's fire slowly shrunk until it matched his.

Teddy raised his eyebrow as he watched a child use an advanced technique, changing a spell while casting it. "Well done!" He praised. "Again!"

As Teddy extinguished his flame, Rina did the same with her own. When he summoned a blaze, she summoned a blaze, either the same size or adjusting hers to equal his. As with the initial test, Teddy had her repeat it with varying sizes until she was able to summon flames equal to his, without adjusting the spell.

"Alright, now to the next technique." Teddy said. "Light the candle again, using the size that we started with."

As he told her, Rina summoned a small flame that took to the wick instantly.

"Now. Change its color to blue." Teddy said, eager to see if she could do it without any other instructions than the ones he taught her already.

Rina stood there, excited to see if she could do what he did, a Master Wizard. She focused hard on the flame, picturing it as he had it in his hand. (Blue...) She thought. (Blue...) As she concentrated hard on the alteration of the fire, the flame flickered and danced on the candle, slowly at first, then violently waving around, changing from its natural color, to varying colors of the rainbow, pink, yellow, green, purple, blue.

"Ease your thoughts, Rina." Teddy cautioned her. "Your mind needs to be calm."

Doing as he said, Rina thought of her family. The good times she had growing up. She smiled as she remembered the dinners her mother would make and the stories her parents would tell them, her eyes closed, she released her hold over the flame, then opened her eyes again. The flame stood there motionless, blue as the ocean.

"What have you done..." Teddy said, stunned at what he was seeing.

"I... I'm sorry..." Rina sniffled, trying not to cry.

"Sorry? You have nothing to be sorry for, girl!" Teddy exclaimed. "Never in my years have I seen this!"

"What did I do?" Rina asked, looking at the flame, realizing that it emitted no heat, yet was still there.

"You... You changed its state." Teddy replied, poking the flame that was now as hard as a rock, shaking his paw as it was still hot to the touch. "This isn't possible."

"Are you okay?" Rina asked, worried that he burned himself.

"I'm fine!" Teddy responded excitedly. "Okay... Okay. I will have to investigate this matter later. You still have yet to accomplish the correct spell."

Teddy took the hard flame and moved it to another table, then summoned a new candle and flame, telling Rina to try again, this time to calm her mind before she attempts to change its color.

As he instructed her, Rina took a deep breath, ridding her mind of all thoughts, exhaling and releasing her magic. Whereas the first flame violently changed from color to color before being changed into a molten blue rock, this one smoothly transferred from its natural hue to that of Teddy's blue.

"Well done! Well done!" Teddy praised her. "Again!" He said, snapping his finger, changing the flame back to its reddish orange color.

The two went on with Rina's training for the remainder of the day. Teddy had her switching between the three techniques until she was able to do them all at once. Summoning a blue flame, the size for a candle, to summoning a fireball, of the same color, the size of her fist. Teddy tried different variations of the spells, all of which Rina was able to accomplish, each new one faster than the one before.

"That's enough magic for today!" Teddy said, filled with pride of the success Rina had in her training, eager to progress into other areas of magic. "Now, I will show you another technique that can help you in all areas of your life." He continued, gesturing for her to follow him.

"What's that?" Rina asked, as they walked out of the secret entrance to his home.

"Easing your mind." Teddy answered, breathing in the fresh air of the night, pointing above them. "We're going up to the top."

"All the way up?" Rina asked, nervous of being so high.

"Yes. There's a path that will take us to the peak that overlooks Kaskia. It's a beautiful sight." Teddy answered, summoning a flame in his hand, lighting their way.

The two walked the path in silence, Rina focusing on where she stepped, trying not to fall. The trail took them almost an hour before they saw the peak. Teddy guided her to a small clearing, enough space for a small house to sit on top of the mountain, walking to the very edge of the peak.

Rina gasped as she looked over the country, seeing lights that Teddy indicated was Toogal and the Capital beyond in the distance.

Amazed how beautiful the stars looked from the top of the mountain. Rina watched as Teddy sat on the edge, legs folded as he did while meditating earlier, and followed his lead.

Teddy told her to breathe and enjoy the view, let the beauty of the world caress her thoughts, soothing her soul. For the first time since she had lost everything she had ever known, Rina felt at peace with the world. Her worries melted away as the cold night air washed over her. She knew in her heart that her parents would be saved, and her brother would awaken.

The following week continued on as her first day. Rina would wake up, check on Aiden and Ellie, who never left his side, then ate breakfast with Teddy and Squishy before continuing her training. Where the first day she studied and learned to control the power she used on her magic, the following days she learned different elements of magic.

Teddy taught her about summoning magic, that any object summoned must come from somewhere, besides the elements such as fire and water, explaining that the candles that he had summoned were from his storage where he had an excess amount of them. He showed her by placing a book on one side of the table and told her how to pull it through the air, opening a portal beneath the item that led to the designated destination.

Teddy showed her how to manipulate water, ice, and the art of healing magic. Every time Teddy tended to Aiden's wound and mental state, Rina assisted him, learning how to heal small wounds. Teddy was very proud of how well she was learning and the rate of her success. By the end of the week, Rina was using magic at an adept's level, something that should have taken her years to accomplish.

"Rina?" Aiden asked as he opened his eyes.

Chapter 18

The sound of Ellie barking excitedly broke Teddy and Rina from their training. The duo rushed out of the library, running in the direction of Aiden's room, knowing that there was only one reason Ellie would be so excited. "He's awake!" Rina cheered.

"Easy, Aiden." Squishy said as Ellie bounced around the room happily, going from licking Aiden on his face to running in circles, wagging her tail.

"What happened?" Aiden asked. "Where's Rina?"

"Aiden!" Aiden heard Rina yell. "Aiden!"

"She's on her way, she's okay." Squishy reassured him just before Rina burst through the door, tackling Aiden on the bed, giving him the biggest hug of his life.

"I was so worried!" She said, smiling as tears rolled down her face, happy that her brother was finally awake and with her once again. "I love you, big brother!"

"I love you too, Rina." Aiden struggled as Rina had a tight grip on him.

"Easy, Rina." Teddy told her as he approached Aiden. "Let me see him."

"Okay Teddy." Rina said, taking a step back.

"Teddy?" Aiden questioned, staring at the old Bermion he assumed was the person they were supposed to meet. "Why do I know that name?"

"You know my name?" Teddy asked, raising his eyebrow as he put a paw to Aiden's forehead.

"Yes. I had so many nightmares, but that name... I remember it from them." Aiden answered.

"What happened in your nightmares?" Teddy asked, moving Aiden forward so he could check his shoulder.

Aiden explained his dreams to Teddy and how the only constant thing in them all were the names Teddy and Cladon, that Cladon wanted all the information he had on the old Bermion and where he was.

"He has gotten far stronger than I feared." Teddy stated.

"Cladon?" Squishy asked.

"Yes, Cladon." Teddy replied, shaking his head. "For him to have had so much power over Aiden, at this distance, proves that his reach is getting farther and farther."

"Is there any way we can stop him from being able to do that?" Rina asked, thinking of her training. "You said almost anything is possible, right?"

"Yes, we can." Teddy answered, smiling at Rina's eagerness to become stronger. "We will go to the library in a few and figure out the right spells to ward us from his gaze."

"How long have I been asleep?" Aiden asked, trying to stand up only to fall into Squishy's arms.

"Easy, Aiden." Squishy told him. "You've been out for over a week."

"Have you found our parents yet?!" Aiden demanded, furious that he's been sleeping for over seven days, seven days that he could have been searching for them.

"Not yet." Rina replied, sadness falling over her face, knowing that Aiden is blaming himself for everything. "Arlington, Grape, and Jr. are out searching for them."

"Let's go help them!" Aiden said, pushing past Squishy only to take three steps before the room spun around him. Determined, Aiden forced himself to keep walking, the room becoming darker. He heard Rina and Squishy, but was unable to make out what they were saying.

"Is he okay?!" Rina asked as Squishy carried Aiden back to his bed.

"He's fine." Teddy replied. "He needs time to recover and he needs to eat."

Teddy gestured for Rina to go to the other side of Aiden's bed, explaining that the two of them are going to perform a spell, blocking Aiden's mind from Cladon. Teddy told Rina that the spell would not have worked before while he was already locked in Cladon's trap and now that he had woken up, they could protect him for now, if he stayed inside the mountain home.

Both Rina and Teddy placed one hand over Aiden's head and the other over his chest. He told Rina to calm her mind and to repeat after him. "No one shall enter your mind or your soul." As they uttered the word soul, a green aura burst into life around Aiden's whole body, bathing the room with its light. "Focus on where our hands are." Teddy told her, guiding her magic to Aiden's chest and head. The green aura slowly moved its way over his heart and head before finally dissipating all together.

"Is that it?" Rina asked, unsure if the spell was in place.

"Yes! Well done child!" Teddy laughed, amazed that she had been able to replicate his magic, augmenting his own spell to banish all signs of Cladon from Aiden. "Well done!"

Teddy excused himself from the room as Squishy, Rina, and Ellie waited for Aiden to wake up again. Only a few hours passed by when his eyes finally opened again. Anticipating his hunger, Squishy already had a plate with bread, cheese cubes, and a couple grapes waiting next to his bed.

"You need to recover." Squishy told him.

"How long will it take?" Aiden asked between bites of the bread and cheese. "I can't just lay here while they're in danger..."

"Give it until tomorrow." Squishy replied. "If you're feeling up to it, then we will start your training."

"Training?!" Aiden said in disbelief. "I don't need training! We need to save them!"

"Aiden..." Rina said. "We're not strong enough yet."

"Besides, we still don't know where they are." Squishy added, handing Aiden a cup of water. "We're still waiting for Grape, Arlington, and Jr. to report back before we can do anything."

"Fine." Aiden said flatly, admitting defeat in the situation.

Aiden did as Squishy said, he waited in bed, laying there thinking about all that had occurred and his dreams. He knew that one day he would meet Cladon face to face, that Cladon wanted it just as much as he did, although, different reasons. He laid there, staring at the wall as his thoughts raced of all the possibilities of what the future holds for him. Despite sleeping for over a week, his eyes became heavy, his thoughts wavered as he drifted back to sleep.

Aiden awoke early in the morning, or so he thought it was, he had no idea the time of day. His room was void of windows, only having a door that was currently shut. As he sat up, Aiden was greeted by Ellie who was laying across his legs.

"Good morning Ellie." He greeted, receiving a yawn and a lazy lick from her on his cheek before she curled back on the foot of the bed. "I can't stay in this bed anymore." He told her as he slowly got out of bed, testing the strength of his legs. Aiden felt the stiffness with each step he took. He walked around the room, stretching his legs and the rest of his body, trying to get it to feel back to normal.

Once Aiden was satisfied he would not collapse again, he opened the door to explore his surroundings. He walked slowly down the hallway, trying not to over exert himself again. He emerged into an open room where he imagined everyone would relax and eat their meals in.

Aiden wondered where he was and why there were no windows in this giant home. A loud noise, from the hallway across the room, caught his attention. It sounded like something crashed and shattered into pieces, curious, Aiden headed in that direction. The closer he got, he started hearing voices, two he recognized, one he thought must belong to the owner of the place he was in.

Aiden walked into a giant room filled with books and a staircase at its center. His gaze followed the direction of the voices, he looked up to the second floor to see Rina, Teddy, and Squishy standing around a table. Aiden watched and listened from below.

"After the water is released, concentrate on holding it still." Teddy directed. "Once you have it still, freeze it."

Aiden wondered what water the old Bermion was talking about, from what he could tell, there was no water near them. His jaw dropped as he saw Teddy raise his hands, a blue aura emanating from them, as water slowly appeared in front of him. At first, it was only a couple sips worth of water, then it was more than enough to fill a jug full of water. Aiden stood there in awe as Teddy held the water, unmoving, floating in air.

"Ready?" Teddy asked.

"Ready." Rina replied.

Teddy let go his hold on the water causing it to drop slightly, before Rina was able to use her own magic to catch it, holding it in air as he did, only in her grasp, the water moved violently within an invisible bubble.

"Good, good." Teddy complimented. "Calm your mind and the water."

Doing as he said, Rina focused on clearing her mind. Aiden could see the strain on her face changed from determination to a calm peaceful state, the water mimicking her expression and becoming still.

"Great!" Teddy exclaimed. "Now, concentrate on freezing it."

Doing as he told her, Rina concentrated on the water, imagining it colder, as cold as ice. She thought of the cold winter nights, feeling the chills going down her spine.

Aiden held his breath as he watched, feeling a chill go down his body as the temperature of the room dropped. Gasping as he watched the water freeze from the inside out, until Rina held a ball of ice in the air. "That's amazing!" He cheered, never seeing Rina control her magic anywhere near what he was seeing now.

Caught off guard, Rina turned to see Aiden below watching. Distracted, Rina released her hold on the ice ball, dropping it to the table, shattering on impact. "Aiden!"

Aiden watched as the ice broke into a million pieces and disappeared as Teddy waved his paw.

Rina greeted Aiden excitedly, hugging him tightly and checking his shoulder, where only a scar remained of his wound. Aiden reassured her that he was feeling better.

"Since you're feeling better." Teddy stated. "Let's head to the training room."

Aiden traded a confused glance with Rina as Squishy and Teddy departed the library.

"We need to see how well you are feeling." Teddy added as the group walked further down the hallway. "It's just up here."

Aiden and Rina followed Teddy into a large circular room, a room that resembled that of an arena. At its center, a sand pit over twenty feet in diameter waited for combatants. Aiden watched as Teddy gestured for Rina to follow him to the seats outside the pit, then pointed for Aiden to go towards its center where Squishy waited.

"Are we sparring?" Aiden asked as he slowly walked towards Squishy.

"Yes." Squishy answered, handing Aiden his shield and a wooden sword. "But we're going to take it easy, for now. We don't want you to over exert yourself."

"Okay..." Aiden replied, placing his shield in his off hand and taking the sword in his main, swinging it around to test its weight.

"Are you ready?" Squishy asked, picking up his own shield and sword from the side of the pit.

Aiden nodded, his shield raised and sword low in his other hand as he waited for Squishy's first move. The duo circled each other cautiously, knowing that they both were skilled fighters, although Aiden was still recovering. Squishy was the first to lose his patience, feigning an attack from above only to attempt to kick his opponent. Aiden caught onto his trick, side stepping the kick to swing his sword sideways.

Squishy quickly used his sword to deflect Aiden's initial attack, and back stepped before Aiden could press him further. Squishy had underestimated Aiden's condition, a mistake he would not make a second time. This time, Aiden did not wait for the Bermion to strike. Aiden covered the gap between them in seconds, jabbing his sword at Squishy, forcing him to dodge the attack. Aiden fought with ferocity, he was upon Squishy before he could recover from the jab, bringing his shield up barely in time to block another attack.

Aiden pressured Squishy with obvious attacks, attacks that Squishy always had barely enough time to dodge, block, or parry. The two moved around the pit as if in an eternal dance. Squishy played Aiden's game, knowing that he would not be able to keep up the assault forever, sooner or later his condition would catch up with him and he would falter. Squishy grinned as he saw Aiden's arm give into the weight of the shield. (He's losing stamina.) He thought as Aiden swung the sword again, forcing Squishy to back step, a step that would prove a fatal mistake.

Before he knew it, Squishy fell backwards, landing on the concrete that rested outside the pit. Aiden was quick to stand over him, his sword pointing down at Squishy's throat.

"Yay!" Rina cheered.

"Well done!" Teddy exclaimed.

"Good job!" Squishy added, as he grasped Aiden's hand, pulling him to his feet. "This whole time... I thought I was wearing you out. You controlled the fight until you could get me to lose my step, didn't you?"

"I knew I couldn't match your strength or stamina." Aiden answered. "I had to try and get you off balance to beat you."

"You were amazing Aiden!" Rina said as she ran towards her brother.

"You two should go get some food and relax." Teddy told Aiden and Rina. "That's all the training for today."

"He's far stronger than he should be." Squishy told Teddy once the children were out of the room. "I could feel it with every strike."

"I think young Rina is to blame for that." Teddy replied, shaking his head in astonishment. "I think her magic has affected his body more than just healing him."

"What do you mean?" Squishy asked.

"I think while she was healing him, she wanted to make his body stronger instead of just recovering." Teddy replied as he looked down at the arena and processed the fight. "I think she actually made his body stronger than a human should be."

"What about his mind?" Squishy questioned, wondering if her magic was so powerful that it could alter a person's physical and mental abilities. "To manipulate a fight in such a way at his age? That's impossible!"

"That is all him." Teddy admitted. "The two of them are an amazing pair."

As the next two weeks went on, the children would wake, eat breakfast, and train. Rina would go with Teddy, Aiden would spar with Squishy. Each proving to be far superior in their skills then the two Bermion could have ever expected. Once Aiden had fully recovered, his strength, speed, and endurance surpassed that of Squishy, the only thing he needed was experience in battle.

Rina's training was going the same as Aiden's. The magic and power that she was able to wield far exceeded that of a child, even that of an experienced wizard. Teddy focused all her training on mastering her control over her thoughts, for fear that she could do anything with her mind if she wanted to. Her power both amazed and frightened him, for if she ever became corrupt the way Cladon had been, the world truly will know fear.

"What's that noise?" Rina asked.

"That's an alarm." Teddy answered. "Someone is coming up the mountain."

Teddy, Squishy, Aiden, Rina, and Ellie all abandoned their training, meeting at the entrance to the lair.

"Who is it?" Aiden asked.

"You'll see." Teddy replied, waving his hand, creating an opening in the mountain to reveal their visitors.

"Grape!" Rina yelled, running towards the purple Bermion. "Arlington! Jr.! You're all back!"

Chapter 19

"Did you find them?!" Aiden asked, hoping they knew the location of their parents.

"We only found your mother." Grape replied solemnly, gently hugging Rina back. "As we thought, She's in Prison City, she's safe for now, locked up, but safe."

"When do we leave?!" Aiden demanded. "The longer we wait, something can happen, or she could be moved!"

"Let us go inside." Teddy answered, gesturing for the group to enter. "We must discuss the situation in more depth, before we go rushing into Prison City. We will rescue her, but we must be smart about how."

"That's not all of it." Jr. added as the group walked through the hallway, heading towards the common area. "From what I gathered up in the capital, they're preparing for war."

"I agree." Grape added as she sat on a cushion. "Prison City also appeared to be preparing for some sort of war. I give it a week, maybe a little more, before they head to Premus."

"Why would they attack Premus?" Rina asked.

"Cladon has always wanted to get rid of Premus." Squishy commented. "This is the battle we've been training for."

"That's good!" Aiden declared excitedly. "When they head out, that would be the best time for us to break mom out!"

"I agree." Teddy stated, scratching at his gray beard. "However, we must warn Loson."

"Who is that?" Aiden asked.

"Loson is the King of Premus." Squishy added.

"What about daddy?" Rina questioned, worried why they could not find him.

"Cladon must have him nearby." Teddy replied. "It's the only thing that makes sense with the attack on Aiden and the fact Jr. and Arlington were unable to find him."

"So, what do we do?" Aiden asked.

"What would you do Aiden?" Teddy asked, raising an eyebrow.

"Hmmm." Aiden said, scratching his head as he thought what his next move would be. "How far are we from Prison City?"

"If we all travel as a group, almost a week." Squishy replied.

"I know they will be looking for Rina, Ellie and me. So, however we travel, the three of us would have to stay out of sight as long as possible." Aiden stated. "I'm assuming they're after you too, Teddy?"

"Yes." Teddy replied, listening to Aiden put together all the pieces.

"So that means all four of us would have to stay hidden. Our best chance with the increased patrols, would be some sort of covered wagon." Aiden added. "That would also slow our trip a lot but would make the timing closer for when we anticipate them leaving for the war."

"Very good." Teddy said. "I agree with that. Grape, Squishy, get some rest, once the sun sets, I want you two to head to Toogal and get us a covered wagon big enough for the four of us to ride in the back."

"What do we do until they return?" Aiden asked.

"Train." Teddy answered. "It will take them at least two days to get to Toogal and meet us at the base of the mountain. We have a day and a half before we leave. Until then, Arlington, Jr., you two will be sparring with Aiden. I will continue to train Rina."

Arlington, Jr., and Aiden headed for the arena as Squishy and Grape left to go rest for the day. The two eyed Aiden as they observed a difference in the boy from the last time they had seen him.

"He's confident." Arlington whispered to Jr. "He seems different."

"He is different." Jr. whispered back.

"Do you guys use swords?" Aiden asked as the trio entered the arena.

"I do." Arlington replied. "He doesn't. He uses his paws."

"Do you want to go first?" Aiden asked Arlington, tossing him the wooden sword that Squishy had used.

"Sure!" Arlington replied, excited to see Aiden's skill. "I won't hold back!"

"Neither will I!" Aiden said just before charging Arlington. Aiden swung his sword sideways, an attack that Arlington easily dodged. Where Squishy had power, Arlington had agility. Aiden quickly changed his tactics.

He waited for Arlington to make his move, grinning, the Kaiine charged Aiden, jumping in the air, sword high above his head, swinging it downward. Aiden grinned back, raising his shield, Aiden blocked the attack and held his ground behind. Slowly, Aiden overpowered the Kaiine, pushing him backwards. Caught by surprise, Arlington stumbled back losing his balance.

Aiden quickly made his counter attack, taking advantage of his opponent's distraction. Aiden slammed his shield in the chest of Arlington, sending the Kaiine tumbling backwards out of the pit.

"When did you get so strong?" Jr. asked, helping Arlington to his feet.

"I don't know." Aiden answered, shrugging his shoulders. "I've just been training with Squishy the past few weeks."

"The last time we saw you... You were so ill." Arlington said, amazed at Aiden's skill. "You fight like your father."

At the statement of his father, Aiden felt a sting in his chest. "Teddy and Rina have been using magic to help my recovery."

"Want to go again?" Arlington asked.

"Sure!" Aiden replied, excited to have a different sparring partner to train with, wanting to experience different fighting styles.

"Rina." Teddy said. "You have the power and skill to do anything your mind can think of. However, you must be careful. Do not try what you are not ready for. Always remember to control your emotions when using magic, if you're not careful, your own magic can destroy you and everyone around you."

"I promise, I will be careful." Rina reassured.

"We may not have much time to train more once we leave here." Teddy told her. "I'm going to teach you one more spell."

"What's that?" Rina asked excitedly to learn a new spell.

"Take this bag." Teddy replied, handing her an empty sack. "These are the books I want you to have, to study, and keep. Over time, you will have your own collection. Place them all inside the bag."

Doing as he instructed, Rina placed all the books inside the bag. "How am I supposed to take these with me? The bag won't close." Rina asked.

"Place your hand on the top of the bag." Teddy instructed. "Now close your eyes and picture a room, a room with no door, no windows, hold that image in your head. Do you have the image?"

"Yes." Rina replied, her eyes closed, hand over the bag, her brow furrowing as she concentrated.

"Now imagine every book you placed in this bag is laying on the floor of that room." Teddy continued. "Well done! Look."

Opening her eyes, Rina gasped as the bag was now empty and was the size of a small pouch. "Where are the books?!"

"In your room." Teddy answered. "When you want a book, reach into the pouch, focus on the image of the room and the books will enter your mind, just think of the book you want, and pull it out of the pouch."

"Really?" She asked, reaching into the bag, gasping as she instantly pulled a book from it. "Can anyone take these books from here? How many books can I keep in the bag?"

"No, Rina. No one can take these books from that bag. Only you." Teddy replied, smiling at her curiosity. "You can only have the number of books that could naturally fit in the bag. If you wish to change a book, simply take one out and place a new one in."

"That's so cool!" Rina said, bouncing with joy. "Wait!? Does this work with other items?!"

"Yes, but you have to be careful what you place in these sacks." Teddy replied. "Books are easy and take less power to use this spell. Other items can be far more draining."

The day went on, Teddy went over details of controlling her energy while casting spells. Aiden, Jr., and Arlington continued sparring until sundown, when Squishy and Grape left for Toogal. The group said their goodbyes and wished the two Bermion good luck on their journey into town, knowing that it was a dangerous place to visit.

That night, the group relaxed in the common room, telling stories, laughing while eating deer jerky, bread, fruit, and drinking juice. Aiden and Rina felt at home for the first time since their world was taken from them. Teddy told them that it may be their last time to really enjoy themselves, for once they leave the following day, they won't have time for having fun.

Aiden dreamt of their mission, finding their mother locked up and rescuing her. He thought of what was needed from him and if he would have the resolve to act. He had become confident in his fighting and his skills with weapons, he was only nervous of fighting for his life, knowing that there were far better warriors than he was.

He had only been in a battle a few times, one of which he was grievously injured, a wound that still haunted him. Most nights, the Iguanians tormented his dreams, not just the ones that gave him his wound, but those he dreamt of when he was under Cladon's spell. Aiden would see his mother twisting into the hideous leather scaled creature as it chased him through his home, scraping the walls with its long-clawed fingers, tearing the house apart.

"Make sure you have all your gear." Teddy reminded the group. "Once we leave, we will not be coming back for a while."

Aiden went to the arena, to gather his shield, sword, and the light armor that Teddy had indicated for him to use. He grabbed a small pouch and headed for the kitchen, taking fruit and bread to carry with him on their journey, knowing they would not have time to search for food.

Rina sat in her room, with Ellie on the bed, reaching into the pouch of books, pulling out a book, then putting it back in, still amazed at what magic could do. She turned her hand over, palm facing upward, and summoned a small flame that floated inches above her hand. Then, just as easy as she had summoned it, she dismissed the flame back from where it came. "Are you ready to go Ellie?" She asked, receiving a bark and a lick on her face, in response.

Rina and Aiden joined the others in the common room, nervous about the mission. They both wanted to rescue their mother but were also scared. This was the first mission they've prepared for, everything up until this point was about survival, about staying alive at all costs. They survived Kaskian soldiers, an unforgiving desert, and worse, Iguanians who seemed immune to magic.

"Everyone ready?" Teddy asked, receiving confirmation from the group. "Then let us head down the mountain."

The group quietly traversed the mountain path that led them to the base and eventually to the site where they had made camp the night Aiden went into his coma. The sun had long since hidden behind the mountains, leaving the group in a limbo of light and dark, getting darker the lower they went. By the time they had reached the bottom, the moon was high in the sky, giving them their only source of light.

"We're almost at the rendezvous point." Teddy stated for the group. "We should be there any minute now."

"What time is it?" Rina asked, rubbing her eyes.

"It's almost midnight." Arlington yawned.

"Is that it?" Aiden asked, pointing to a clearing with a small fire pit in the middle.

"Yes, that's it." Teddy answered. "Everyone, get some rest, we will need it."

"Where's Squishy and Grape?" Rina questioned as she looked around the campsite.

"They should arrive before morning." Arlington explained, placing his paw on her shoulder.

"What about if a patrol comes by?" Aiden asked, unsure who's supposed to keep watch.

"Do not worry." Teddy reassured. "I have a cloaking spell around us. It will deter anyone from finding us."

Chapter 20

"Squishy, Grape, take off your armor and put it in the wagon." Teddy instructed. "You must not look aggressive."

"The sun is rising." Arlington pointed out.

"Jr., Arlington, go and scout ahead." Teddy ordered the two Kaiine. "Aiden, Rina, Ellie, hop in the back of the wagon."

The group quickly loaded their gear in the back of the wagon and then they followed Teddy's instructions. Aiden, Rina, and Ellie jumped in the back of the wagon where all the gear was piled up. Grape and Squishy hopped on the front of the carriage, wearing only leather tunics and pants, grabbing the reins, and ushered the horses to be on their way. Aiden looked out the back of the wagon, watching Arlington and Jr. disappear into the woods.

"Will they be ok?" Rina asked, pointing at Jr. and Arlington as they vanished from their sight.

"They will be fine." Teddy replied. "So will Squishy and Grape."

"How come you don't use a spell to make the whole wagon invisible to everyone?" Aiden asked.

"Rina, do you know the answer?" Teddy asked, curious to see if she could answer her brother's question.

"I think..." Rina said, thinking back on everything Teddy had taught her. "It takes less energy to mask the opening back here than it would to completely vanish the whole wagon while it moves."

"Very good!" Teddy replied cheerfully.

"Oh." Aiden added, feeling annoyed that he didn't understand magic the way his sister did. "So, what are we to do while we ride back here?"

"Well." Teddy said. "As long as we're quiet, we can discuss anything that you two would like to know."

"Why are you hiding back here with us?" Aiden asked bluntly, wanting to know why the old Bermion was hiding from the King of Kaskia.

"As you know, I am a Wizard." Teddy replied. "That alone makes me wanted by Cladon."

"That can't be the whole truth." Rina added, also curious.

"You both are very observant for your age." Teddy sighed. "Very well. I knew Cladon years ago. I fought for Premus in the first war, he fought for Kaskia."

"Wasn't the first war a really long time ago?" Rina interrupted.

"Yes, I am very old Rina." Teddy admitted. "Bermion's live longer than humans, but I am indeed far older than most Bermion's."

"Then you know how Cladon stayed alive so long?" Aiden asked.

"No, my long life is not due to my own magic." Teddy replied, shaking his head and waving his paw to end the questions on the subject.

"So, he just knows you from the war and wants your magic?" Aiden questioned suspiciously.

"More or less." Teddy shrugged. "Next to him, I am the second strongest magic wielder in the land. He doesn't want anyone to have magic that rivals his own."

The trio fell into silence, having many things on their minds as they rode in the back of the wagon, feeling every bump in the dirt road they traveled. Many times, the group had been stopped along their journey. Every time the Kaskian soldiers had looked in the back of the wagon, Aiden and Rina held their breath, their hearts racing with anticipation, yet each time, the soldiers signaled for them to keep going, satisfied the wagon was empty. Teddy assured them each time that they would be safe from prying eyes.

The group pressed on as the sun rose high in the sky and began its descent. They kept traveling well into the night, only stopping once Arlington and Jr. reported finding a sizable clearing not too far off the road. As soon as they stopped for the night, Squishy and Grape found spots around the wagon to rest for the night. Aiden and Rina stayed inside the carriage with Ellie as Teddy walked into the woods to meditate, reassuring them that their camp is protected from the soldiers. Arlington and Jr. found large branches in the trees to sleep on, keeping an eye out for any threats from above the group.

"I feel like he's hiding something from us about Cladon." Aiden whispered to Rina. "He knows more about the King."

"What do you think it is?" Rina replied as she fiddled with her bag.

"I don't know." Aiden shrugged. "I just don't like that he's hiding something, and that he's so old and claims he didn't cast a spell to live that long."

"Maybe someone cursed him?" Rina asked as she dug through her pouch, trying to find a book to read before she goes to sleep for the night.

"How..." Aiden questioned, watching Rina pull a book from a pouch smaller than the book itself. "Magic... Never mind."

"This... I didn't put this in there." Rina muttered to herself. "It's a journal."

"What?" Aiden asked.

"Nothing." Rina replied, putting the journal back into the bag and bringing out another book. "That's the one I was looking for!"

"What are you doing?" Aiden asked, curious as she flipped through the book.

"Teddy has techniques in here to try and control my magic." Rina replied. "Fire. Water. Earth. Wind."

Aiden watched stunned as Rina summoned elements each time she said their name. First a flame blazed above her hand, then a sphere of water formed where the fire had been. When she said Earth, the water changed and grew harder, more dirt like before disintegrating all together when she uttered wind, a visible gust burst out from within the ball of dirt that was in her hand, circling as if a small pet tornado.

He didn't know much about magic, but Aiden felt like she was doing something far more advanced then what the book told her. Not only did she summon the elements in her hand, she changed them from one to another.

"I wonder." Rina muttered to herself. "Lightening."

As soon as she voiced the word, thunder shook the earth and the sky as a lightning bolt flowed around her hand the way a serpent slithers around a branch.

"Earth!" Rina quickly said, summoning dirt that slowly encased the lightning, leaving a bracelet of grime around her hand.

"How...." Aiden stuttered, eyes wide as he witnessed Rina controlling lightning.

"I... I don't know!" Rina replied, staring at the dirt around her hand. "Go away..." With her command, the dirt vanished from her hand.

"Are you guys ok?" Teddy asked, peeking into the back of the wagon.

"Yes... Yes..." Rina replied, still shaken by the lightning that had been wrapped around her wrists only moments before.

"Why didn't you tell him?" Aiden asked once Teddy was out of earshot.

"I promised I would be careful..." Rina replied. "That was not careful of me!"

"It will be okay." Aiden reassured, trying to console her.

"There's so much I don't know about magic!" She said, shaking her head as she shoved the book back into the pouch.

Aiden and Rina both laid down, not wanting to think about what was to come. They both knew that they would either see their mother the next night or die trying. Rina fell asleep, lost in thoughts that invaded her dreams, turning them into nightmares.

"You're my biggest regret!" Teddy yelled as lightning flashed in the distance, thunder echoing behind them.

"You should be proud of me!" Cladon retorted, raising his hands in the air as rain drenched over him. "I did what you never could! I broke us free of Premus! You know what Trench would have done to us!"

"I never wanted you to lose yourself..." Teddy replied solemnly, shaking his head. "I never wanted you to hurt the innocent."

"There must be a sacrifice for power!" Cladon replied. "You could never accept that..."

"You can't justify what you have done!" Teddy yelled as rain poured down from the heavens.

Cladon paced across the tower, water dripping from his body as a storm berated them, winds threatening to whisp them up off into the sky. Back towards Teddy, Cladon looked down over the battle below, his castle was under siege, his empire on the brink of destruction. He thought about all the sacrifices he had made in his life, the lives he had taken, Cladon was not ready to give up, not when he was so close to attaining his goals. "Give her to me!"

"You can't have her!" Teddy yelled back, pointing behind him to Rina.

"You don't understand!" Cladon bellowed, never taking his gaze off the battle below. "Her life is a necessary sacrifice..."

"There's no such thing as a necessary sacrifice!" Teddy replied, driving his staff into the stone floor of the tower. "You will not take her from me!"

"Have it your way!" Cladon replied, looking over his shoulder as a lightning grew out of his arm, slithering its way towards his hand. Thunder boomed across Kaskia as Cladon thrust his arm towards Teddy, causing the bolt to leap from the mad King, slicing through the air in the direction of the old Bermion.

"No!" Rina yelled, causing Teddy to look back at her, confusion showing across his face.

"What are you doing here?" Teddy asked as the bolt of lightning inched its way closer to him.

Looking down, Rina saw a human girl lying unconscious on the ground. Time moved slow as she processed what was happening.

The girl on the ground looked a lot like her, only older. Her stomach tightened as she tried to figure out what she was looking at.

Time seemed to pause as she focused on the situation, trying to figure out where she was, how they ended up on the top of a tower. She could see rain drops floating still in the air as she tried to think of the last thing she remembered, thunder roared above her as she heard Teddy yell at her.

"Wake up!" Teddy shouted at Rina, breaking her from her thoughts. Rina looked up at the old Bermion just in time to hear him yell wake up once more before the bolt of lightning struck him in his chest, sending Teddy flying off the tower's edge, a look of sadness spread across his face as he fell to the ground below.

"Wake up Rina!" Aiden said, waking her from her nightmare. "Are you okay?"

"I... I don't know." Rina replied, shaking from what she saw in her dream. "I... don't know..."

Chapter 21

"Are you two okay?" Teddy asked as the wagon bounced on the dirt road. "You seem on edge this morning."

"We're okay." Aiden replied, glancing at Rina who looked completely out of it. "Right Rina?"

"Huh?" Rina answered, shaking her head, oblivious of the conversation. "Oh! Yes, we're okay Teddy."

"Okay. Well, we should be getting close." Teddy stated. "Once we're near enough, Squishy and Grape will stop and we all will go over the plan."

Rina and Aiden sat in silence, Aiden thinking about what sort of nightmare Rina had that affected her so much. He had never seen her so withdrawn from the world.

He thought about his own nightmares and how Cladon tormented his dreams, wondering if the mad King could have possibly entered her dreams as well, then quickly dismissing it, knowing that Teddy has them both protected from Cladon's gaze. Aiden watched as she stared out the back of the wagon, obviously troubled by something she dreamt about.

Rina stared into the distance, trying to piece together her dream, if it was a dream at all or a premonition of the future. She thought about how Cladon talked as if he was on the same side as Teddy. Although her dream made her doubt him, Rina still trusted Teddy, the old Bermion in her dream sacrificed himself to protect her, something she felt that the real Teddy would do without hesitation.

Her dream reinforced the thoughts that he was hiding something from them, something from everyone, about his past and relationship to the evil Sorcerer.

"We're stopping." Teddy told Aiden and Rina. "Come outside."

"Where are we?" Aiden asked as he hopped out of the wagon, only to see trees surrounding them.

"Just through those trees is Prison City." Arlington answered, pointing to the west.

"What's the plan?" Jr. asked.

"There will be Soldiers everywhere, even though the majority should be leaving for war." Teddy explained. "There will still be a large amount that we need to avoid."

"There's a city around the actual prison, which is why they call it Prison City." Squishy added. "Most the soldiers live in the city and work within the prison."

"Grape and Squishy will continue to steer the wagon, disguised as traders." Teddy stated. "The four of us will stay hidden until we find an inn. Arlington, Jr., you two will have to wait until nightfall, scout the prison and make your way to us."

"Once we're at the inn, Squishy and I will get a room. Teddy is going to cloak you three." Grape added, pointing at Aiden, Rina, and Ellie. "And take you to the room, where Arlington and Jr. will meet us."

"Once we all are there." Teddy said. "We will figure out the best way to enter the prison and get your mother out, any questions?"

"No." The group replied in unison, all knowing what needed to be done.

"Then until we reach the room, everyone must remain silent." Teddy told them.

Arlington and Jr. disappeared into the trees as Squishy ushered the wagon back on the road to their destination. Aiden sat in the back, anxious, knowing that he was so close to his mother yet unable to run up to her, wanting, more than anything, to be held in her arms, to be told everything will be okay.

Despite how much he appeared to be stronger than he was the day he lost his parents, Aiden was on the verge of breaking down at any moment. He silently promised his father that he would do everything he could to keep Rina safe and to rescue their mother, that he would stay strong until the day comes when the time was right for him to let his emotions free.

The closer they got to the city, Aiden could hear the chaos of people moving about, working, talking, laughing, all as one loud living sound. He wondered how anyone could ever live in such a deafening place, missing the quiet woods where he grew up.

"Halt!" Aiden heard a voice shout. "What's your business here, Bermion?"

"We're here to trade and get supplies to sell to surrounding villages." Squishy replied.

Aiden and Rina froze, tense, waiting for the soldier to reply.

"What's in the back?" The soldier asked.

Aiden and Rina fought back panic, thinking that it was all going to be over, for sure they would be found in the back with so many soldiers around. Dread filled them as they waited for the soldiers to inspect the wagon.

"Supplies. You can see for yourself." Grape replied.

"Go check it out!" The soldier yelled to those under his command.

Aiden and Rina watched as four soldiers walked behind the wagon, peering in at the group. Ellie's hair stood on edge, growling softly. Teddy raised his hand and told the soldier all is good.

"All is good." The soldier told his superior.

"Don't cause any problems! We're watching you Bermions!" The soldier told Squishy and Grape as he signaled that they could proceed.

"How..." Aiden started to ask Teddy, only to be shushed by the old Bermion. They had only passed the gate, not safe yet.

Aiden observed the city as they traveled down cobblestone streets. The city had a dark, gloomy look to it. Almost as if it rested in a permanent dusk. He saw people on horses traveling behind them, amazed that they did not see them in the back of the wagon.

He saw all types of shops littering the streets, smoke strewing from chimneys across the city. He thought that if the day came when he was not wanted, he would enjoy exploring such a place, although he would never want to live in a loud city. Aiden watched as they passed a group of soldiers marching with half a dozen people in chains, wondering what crimes the prisoners had committed.

As the wagon halted, Aiden and Rina held their breath, scared that they may have been found and would be surrounded by soldiers any second.

"It's okay." Teddy whispered to them. "We're at the Inn. Squishy and Grape should be heading inside to get a room."

A few moments later, Squishy walked around the back of the wagon, signaling that they were ready to head into the room. Teddy climbed out of the wagon first, observing the surroundings. Once satisfied, he gestured for the kids and Ellie to follow. "Stay close." He whispered as they walked their way into the inn, Grape in the front of them with Squishy covering their rear.

This had been the second inn Aiden had seen, as with the first, the lower floor was a gathering place for people to eat and drink, however, this inn was far scarier than that of the first. The inn was filled with soldiers in full armor and varying weapons at their hips or strapped to their backs. Aiden was amazed that no one seemed to notice them as they traversed the crowd, towards the stairs that would lead them to their room above.

"We're free to talk now." Teddy said as Squishy shut the door to their room. "The room is warded so no one can hear us outside."

"What do we do now?" Aiden asked, anxiously pacing the room.

"We rest and wait." Squishy replied. "Nothing we can do until nightfall."

"And we have to wait for Arlington and Jr. to join us." Grape added.

"I'm nervous..." Rina stated, unable to hide her fears any longer.

"Everything will be okay." Grape reassured her, kneeling next to Rina.

"Everything will go as planned." Teddy added, patting Rina on her head. "Do not worry."

"What about after?" Aiden asked, still pacing the room nervously. "Where are we going?"

"The hideout in the desert." Squishy replied. "It's not too far from here, it is our best hope to escape from the soldiers and stay hidden."

"Once we are there, we will probably spend a few days, if not longer." Teddy added. "After that, we will have to figure out the next move."

Aiden continued to pace the room while they waited for the sun to set. He played every scenario he could think of. Worst case, they reach their mother to find out that she is not alive, or, the information they had was wrong and she was no longer being held within the prison and taken with the army up north.

For the worst-case scenario, there was not much he could do, besides prepare mentally as best he could. If they took her up north, that would mean chasing and fighting an army to get her back, which had very little odds of success. The best option he could think of, would be to go to Premus and help them, using an army to fight an army, and hope to find a way to save her during the war.

Rina sat on the bed, holding Ellie in her arms, wanting comfort from her dark thoughts. Ellie licked her face gently, trying to ease her mind as best she could. Rina knew they would be fighting soon, something she was not fully prepared for, remembering how Aiden got hurt by the Iguanians and how useless she was in helping him. Shaking her head to clear the thoughts from her mind, she looked over to see her brother pacing the room, just as lost in thoughts as she was.

Grape and Squishy stood guard, patiently waiting for Arlington and Jr. to show up. Both mentally preparing for the battle to come. Knowing that the mission will be risky, that there is a chance not all of them will make it out alive. Even if most of the soldiers of the city were gone, there is still a huge presence within the prison walls, a number that their group would have trouble fighting off if it came to it.

Teddy sat in the middle of the room, legs crossed as he meditated, concentrating on their mission. He mentally went over a checklist, making sure they had everything they needed, reciting spells in his head, preparing which ones would be best to use for the situation they were going to be in. "They are here." He stated without opening his eyes.

"Arlington and Jr.?" Rina asked.

"Yes." Grape replied, opening the window for the two to climb through.

"We have good news and bad news." Jr. said, after swinging in through the window.

"What's the bad news?" Squishy asked.

"Cladon's army is not going through Osion to Premus." Arlington answered. "They're heading north, to Dealay, and they're building a bridge wide enough for their army to cross the river. Their first target being the city of Loson."

"Why would he do that?" Squishy asked.

"Because Premus would see them coming if they went through Osion, and the bridge down there is not big enough for his army to cross efficiently." Teddy answered, standing up from his meditation. "That must be why Cladon took their father up north."

"What do you mean?" Rina questioned, not following what they were talking about.

"Your father is a master blacksmith, if not the best one in Kaskia." Grape replied. "With Cladon's magic, and your fathers craft, they could build a bridge without Premus noticing it."

"That is very troubling." Teddy stated, walking to the window, gazing up at the stars.

"Then what's the good news?" Aiden asked.

"The majority of the soldiers in town." Jr. replied. "They're moving out, as we speak, to join the army up north."

"So, that means the prison has the only soldiers we have to worry about." Arlington added excitedly.

Chapter 22

"We should go in quick and take out everyone in our way!" Arlington argued, pointing in the direction of the prison.

"If we do that then we risk not getting to their mother!" Jr. retorted, throwing his paws in the air. "We can't just go in recklessly!"

"The faster we get in there the quicker we can get her out!" Arlington snapped.

"Enough!" Teddy interjected. "We must figure out all options and go with the one with the best chance of success."

"What did you find out about the prison?" Squishy asked.

"There are four towers, on each corner of the prison." Arlington stated. "Each tower has two to three guards."

"There's also patrols of two that travel between the towers." Jr. added. "There's at least five guards at the gate. From what we could tell, there's cages all throughout the prison. Two stories tall."

"How did you get all this information?" Aiden asked.

"There's a tavern not too far from the south eastern tower." Jr. replied. "From the tip of the roof, we could see into the prison."

"Is it in shooting distance for your bow?" Aiden questioned.

"Hmm." Jr. replied, scratching his chin. "It should be, why?"

"Do we have any kind of rope?" Aiden continued to ask, a plan forming in his mind.

"Yes." Grape replied, eyeing Aiden curiously.

"From that roof, you could see the guard's locations on the tower and the walls, if you watch from there and signal to us from below the tower." Aiden speculated. "We could climb the tower and take out the guards above, right?"

"It is... Possible." Jr. answered.

"From there, you could also cover our retreat, right?"

"That would be no problem!" Jr. agreed.

"What else?" Teddy asked Aiden, wanting to hear the rest of his plan.

"Once we're in the tower, we would have to take out the patrol's as fast as possible." Aiden added. "Then have Arlington keep watch from the walls. If I was Cladon, I would have my most wanted prisoners towards the center of the prison. So once the patrols are down, it's just a matter of searching as quietly as we can."

"That sounds... Doable." Arlington stated.

"Agreed." Jr. replied.

"Squishy? Grape? Any concerns?" Teddy asked. "Rina?"

"No." Grape and Squishy replied.

"What about Ellie?" Rina asked, petting Ellie on her head.

"I can carry her up." Squishy answered.

"The plan sounds good." Teddy stated. "Jr., I want you on the roof, watching the patrols and signaling to us. Arlington, once we clear the tower, you stay there and cover us from within the prison. Grape and Ellie will take the lead once we're below, then Aiden, myself, and Rina. Squishy will bring up the rear."

"What about the prisoners?" Aiden asked. "Once they see us, they're most likely going to get loud and draw attention."

"I will handle that." Teddy replied. "I will shield us from their eyes. Any other questions?"

"No." The group replied in unison.

With the plan settled, the group prepared to head out. Arlington and Jr. jumped out the window, keeping watch from below on the cobblestone street. Teddy jumped down after them, using magic to slow his fall so he would land gently behind them.

Once he was on the ground, Teddy opened a pouch on his belt, pulling a staff with a purple gem resting at its tip. Grape picked up Rina and jumped next, having the most grace out of the group as she always did.

"Are you okay?" Squishy asked Aiden, seeing him hesitate.

"I'm nervous." Aiden replied. "What if this doesn't work?"

"Do not worry, everything will be fine. You have the best with you and we will save your mother." Squishy promised.

Nodding without any other words, Aiden jumped out the window, rolling when he landed behind the group.

"Ellie, are you ready?" Squishy asked her, receiving his answer when Ellie jumped in his arms. Squishy carefully jumped from the window, with Ellie, landing behind Aiden.

"Everyone ready?" Teddy whispered.

Jr. and Arlington jogged, on opposite sides, down the street, pausing at an intersection, peeking around the corner for any threats. With no one in sight, Jr. signaled to the group that it was clear and to follow him to their left. As before, Arlington ran down the other side of the street across from Jr., both watching out for any signs of remaining Kaskian Soldiers in the city. The streets were deserted from all its inhabitants, all of whom were inside their houses resting peacefully.

As the group traversed the city, Teddy held a protective spell over them, keeping them hidden from any restless citizens peering from their homes. Rina walked with Aiden and Teddy down the center of the street with Ellie following right behind them, and Squishy behind her. Grape stayed near Jr. and Arlington, only a few paces behind them, keeping an eye out for anything the two did not see.

She was trained for stealth and had the best chance of taking out an enemy without making a sound. Aiden did everything he could to keep his mind focused and not dwell on everything that could go wrong. His nerves fighting to take over his body, his mind telling him how everything was going to fail because of him. He shook his head, removing the negativity from his mind and refocused on what was ahead of them.

Aiden watched as Arlington gave a signal to Jr., who then nodded as the pair simultaneously shot arrows from around the corner, that was followed by two quiet thuds. Grape raised her paw for the group to halt as they waited for the Kaiine's sign. Arlington and Jr. briefly disappeared around the corner to momentarily return, giving the all clear. Grape briefly talked with them before the two went further down the street they had fired the arrows down.

"There was a patrol and there's probably more." Grape stated when she walked up to Teddy. "They hid their bodies in an alley. We must hurry before they're found."

The group pressed on as the moon lit the sky above. The city gave off an eerie feel in the cold night. Aiden quietly cursed himself, thinking he should have known there would be patrols left in the city. His doubt creeped back into his thoughts, feeling him with dread.

He felt as if there were eyes watching them from the shadows, that at any moment, a creature from his nightmares would burst out and attack them. He shook his head, ridding his mind from such thoughts, knowing that it was only his imagination, that only human soldiers stood between them and his mother.

Again, they came across a patrol, as before, the two Kaiine dispatched them with ease and disposed of the bodies. Rina felt sorrow in her heart, that they had taken the lives of the soldiers who were only doing their job. For all she knew, they didn't want to be there patrolling the city, or working for the king, that maybe they only did the job because they were threatened by the Cladon.

With each soldier they crossed, Rina silently apologized to them, hoping they would find better in the next life. Rina did not want the life where she had to take the lives of others, she felt that everyone deserved to be happy and enjoy what the world has to offer. She made a quiet vow to herself, once the war was done, she would do everything she could to end the suffering caused by war and help all people of the world live as happy as she had with her family and that she would only take a life if there were no other options.

"The tavern is still open." Jr. told Teddy. "We should still be good to use the roof, just might have some interference on the way out."

Jr. shot an arrow with a rope tied to the other end, at the roof of the tavern. After yanking the rope, making sure it was secure, Jr., quietly made his way up the wall, towards the top. Aiden watched as the Kaiine made it to the rooftop and pulled the arrow from where it penetrated the tavern.

The group silently made their way to the base of the tower and waited for Jr. to fire his arrow with the rope, signaling for them to climb the tower. It felt like an eternity to Aiden, while they waited for the signal, a signal he dreaded would not come, fearing that the information they had given was wrong, that there were far more soldiers within the prison then they thought, making the mission impossible to save his mother. Or worse, that his plan was a bad idea. There were so many things that could go wrong that troubled his mind, making him doubt himself more and more the closer they got to his mother.

The sound of an arrow piercing into the stone above, broke Aiden from his thoughts. Looking up, he saw that Grape was already making her way up the side of the tower, to finally disappear over the ledge above. Only moments later, Aiden heard a single thud from overhead, a sound that sent chills through his body as he waited for another, knowing there should have been at least two thuds if not three. (Did they find her?) He thought.

Chapter 23

"There's the signal." Squishy whispered as he saw Jr. gesture to them.

Without a word, Arlington slung his bow across his back and began his ascent up the rope, only taking him a few seconds to climb to the top of the tower. Squishy was the next to climb the tower, holding Ellie against his chest with a rope around the two.

"You're next." Teddy said, patting Aiden on his shoulder. "Do not worry, stay focused, and everything will be alright."

Taking a deep breath, Aiden began climbing the rope. Sword in its sheath, shield on his back, he thought about the fights to come, mentally preparing himself. Aiden imagined using his sword to take down his enemies. Every fight he has been in so far, has always been in self-defense.

This time, however, he was the one assaulting others. Although he did not like the idea of taking a life, he knew that if it came to those he cared about, he would not hesitate to slay an enemy in his way. Looking up, Aiden saw Squishy reaching down to help him over the edge of the tower.

Aiden looked around the tower, seeing two unconscious guards resting in a corner, out of sight. Grape stood at one opening to the north wall, Arlington stood at the opening to the west wall, both watching for the patrols. Ellie stood watching over the unconscious guards, he wondered why she left them alive.

Glancing backwards, Aiden saw Squishy assisting Rina to the top of the tower, followed by Teddy who immediately walked towards the two unconscious forms, kneeling next to them and placing one paw over their foreheads.

"Incoming." Arlington told the group, indicating that the west patrol was on their way.

"Everyone, stay hidden." Squishy replied. "When they get close, take them out."

Aiden watched as Arlington stood with his back against the stone doorway, ears twitching. He wondered just how good the Kaiine hearing was. Before Aiden knew it, Arlington had moved into the doorway, releasing an arrow that was followed by two thuds. "Two?" He muttered to himself, then looked across to where Jr. was standing on the roof, bow drawn as if he just shot his own arrow. (That's why they make such a good team for tracking... They can communicate from so far away) He thought.

"Aiden!" Squishy said, breaking him from his thoughts. "Help bring the bodies in!"

Squishy and Aiden quickly went on the south wall to drag the two bodies back into the cover of the tower as Arlington and Jr. continued to cover for any further enemies.

"Got it!" Teddy exclaimed triumphantly. "Your mother is here, and I know where!"

"How do you know where she is?" Aiden asked.

"I read their thoughts, not an easy task." Teddy replied. "She is being guarded by seven soldiers, near the center of the prison."

"I should be able to cover you most of the way." Arlington stated, looking over the prison from the tower.

"Incoming!" Grape told the group, indicating that the patrol from her side was nearing.

Where Arlington and Jr. took out the guards from the west wall, from a distance, Grape made a noise to lure the guards into the tower where she and Squishy quickly dispatched them before they knew what happened.

"We should be clear from any interruptions on this tower now." Squishy said.

"Then let's get moving!" Grape replied, waiting by the staircase that led down the tower from within.

Ellie quickly ran to her side, sniffing the air before heading down the spiral staircase with Grape. Ellie stopped half way down the stairs, fur standing on edge, growling quietly. Grape looked below, seeing a soldier standing by the door that led to the prison. The man looked bored, leaning against the wall, back towards the stairs. Grape signaled for the group to wait as she quickly ran down towards the guard, who never heard her coming. Aiden watched as she reached around, covering his mouth with her paw, as her dagger dug deep into his back.

Aiden and Squishy helped to move the man's body out of sight, while Grape peered out the doorway, observing their surroundings. "Teddy, you're up."

Glancing out the door, Teddy saw cells out in the open, one two story row against the tower wall, facing the center of the prison. Across from them, rested multiple rows of two stories cells that went down towards the opposite wall. Teddy imagined the whole prison and all its cells, he closed his eyes and focused on all the inhabitants of the prison, except their mother, and whispered a single word. "Sleep."

Aiden glanced out of the doorway and watched as any of the prisoners who were awake, standing at the bars of their cells, turned and walked away, assuming they were going to their bed to sleep as Teddy had said.

"Done." Teddy replied only moments later. "They're all sleeping now."

Grape cautiously crept out of the tower, Ellie at her side, and walked towards the first aisle of cells, seeing that they did not go all the way to the other wall, but had a dead-end part way down. Towards the middle of the first aisle, stood a single guard who was looking into one of the cells, tapping the bar. Grape raised her paw and pointed in the man's direction, who had an arrow plunge into his chest a second later.

Teddy indicated for them to keep moving, taking out each enemy that would pose a threat to them, either ahead or after they would pass them. The ones that Arlington was unable to shoot, Grape had quietly snuck up on them as she did the tower guards and dispatched each one. The prison was a large place with many aisles housing many prisoners and worse, had many guards.

"That one." Teddy said quietly, pointing to the next aisle. "We need to go down that one."

Grape and Ellie stopped just before the opening to the aisle and peeked down to see what waited for them. Where the previous rows had only one soldier in them, this one had three. Grape thought about the best way to take out the three of them without making any sounds or raising the alarm that they were there. They were currently a few paces away and walking in the opposite direction of them.

Ellie nudged Grape in her leg, giving her a quiet yip of encouragement. Trusting in her, Grape quietly ran into the aisle, Ellie a few steps ahead of her. Ellie was faster than the Bermion, she was near the first guard. Once she was in reach, Ellie gave a faint bark, barely loud enough for the guard to hear, who turned to see Ellie lunging for him.

Ellie landed square on his chest, her jaw closed in around the soldier's throat, keeping him from screaming. The two remaining guards turned as they heard the first fall; before they knew it, Grape had thrown one of her daggers at the nearest soldier, killing him instantly, then thrusted her second dagger into the chest of the last soldier. Ellie and Grape had finished all three soldiers without alerting anyone else in the prison.

"Make a left up there." Teddy stated as the group ended up at a three-way intersection.

Grape glanced down the left, seeing another three soldiers, all of whom were half way down the aisle and walking towards the group. Looking behind her, she saw another three walking to their right, away from them.

"Teddy, Rina, we will need help with these three, to keep them quiet." Grape whispered quietly. "Squishy, Aiden, once we take out these three, I need you two to take out the other three down there."

"One. Two. Go!" Grape said, giving the signal to attack.

Ellie and Grape were upon the first soldier, Ellie knocking the man down as she had done the other, Grape coming up behind her to stab him, finishing him off. Teddy cast a spell on the second soldier, who attempted to shout to alert others, but had lost his voice. After she had killed the first man, Grape had moved onto the one with no voice, easily dodging his attack and forcing her daggers into his upper body.

Rina had the last soldier, she whispered "Freeze." Ice crept up around the man's throat, slowly making its way across his body before completely encasing the man, freezing him in place.

Teddy glanced down at Rina, nodding in approval that she had done what she needed to do. Rina whispered an apology to the fallen men, feeling sorrow that they had to die to save her mother. She glanced back in time to see Squishy and Aiden catch up to the other three soldiers, one was already dead, the other two turned in time to see Squishy's hammer come down on one of their skulls and Aiden's sword penetrating the chest of the other. The group left the bodies where they landed and continued their search for Brittany.

"Her cell, with the seven guards, should be around that corner." Teddy whispered, pointing ahead of them.

Grape took a quick glance to see what waited for them. "There's at least ten guards from what I can see, maybe more." Grape stated, shaking her head at the amount of enemies waiting for them.

"More must have joined them." Teddy sighed, frustrated that the intel he had gathered turned out to be wrong.

"I have an idea, what if you two go to the second floor." Aiden said, pointing at Teddy and Rina. "And wait for Grape to lure them over here. Squishy, you Ellie and I will wait for them to get closer before we attack."

"That could work." Grape replied.

"Sounds good to me." Teddy answered. "There was a staircase just back there, come Rina."

"We're almost there." Squishy told Aiden, placing his paw on his shoulder. "You've done an amazing job."

"They're ready." Grape said, pointing at Teddy and Rina who stood on the floor above. "Are you two ready?"

"Yes." Squishy and Aiden replied.

Aiden watched as Grape walked out in plain sight for the soldiers to see. She walked towards a cell and peered in, as if she was lost.

"Halt!" A soldier yelled as the group ran towards her, swords drawn and ready to attack. "How did you get in here?!"

"Me?" Grape asked nonchalantly, glancing over her shoulder at the guards.

"Yes you!" The leader of the guard replied, as they began to surround her, oblivious of Squishy, Aiden, and Ellie who were now behind them.

Turning to face the group, Grape pulled out her daggers, giving the signal for the others to strike as she attacked the nearest soldier, killing him instantly. Aiden was the second to attack, stabbing his sword in the back of a soldier, then using his shield to bash another in the back of the head, sending him to the ground.

Five of the remaining soldiers turned to face Aiden, Squishy, and Ellie, while the other two, faced Grape. "Sound the alarm!" The leader yelled as the soldiers charged.

Rina summoned a fireball in her hand and sent it flying into the leader's chest, sending him flying into the cell behind him. Teddy used magic to bring roots through the stone floor, entangling the guard's feet, causing them to be distracted as the others finished them off easily. Grape threw a dagger into a man's face, then thrust the other dagger into the last guard's neck.

Squishy swung his giant hammer in a sideways motion, slamming it into the torso of one soldier, crushing him into the remaining two that faced Aiden and Squishy. Ellie jumped on top of the only soldier who was still conscious, who was trying to escape, pinning him to the ground. Aiden walked up to him and stabbed him in the chest, killing him mercifully.

"Incoming!" Teddy shouted as he saw two archers let loose their arrows.

Aiden quickly rushed to Ellie's side, raising his shield to protect her from the oncoming assault. Squishy and Grape took cover behind the cells from where they came. Rina was the one to react, after seeing what Teddy had done with the roots, she too did the same, except for her roots, they completely wrapped around the archers and dragged them underground, leaving no trace behind.

"We have to move!" Aiden yelled as an alarm blared around the prison. Looking in the distance, Aiden saw the person who he came to rescue, standing in a cell, hands around the bars, staring back at him. "Mom!" Aiden raced towards her, all thoughts left his mind, the only thing that mattered was his mother.

"Aiden?" Brittany stuttered, unsure if he was truly there. "How?"

"We're here to get you out mom!" Aiden replied as the rest of the group caught up, Ellie barking excitedly.

"Stand back." Teddy told the group as he waved his hand at the door to the cell, causing the lock to turn bright red before melting away completely. "We must hurry."

With the door open, Aiden, Rina, and Ellie ran inside the cell, hugging their mother tightly as all of them had tears streaming down their faces. "But how?" Brittany asked, surprised that they were safe.

"There's no time for this." Grape stated. "We have to leave this place before we all end up living here."

Brittany eyed her saviors, unsure what to make of the Bermians and the situation that her children must be in to end up with such a group. "They're right, let's go kids." Brittany agreed, kneeling to pick up a quiver and bow that an archer dropped.

"They're coming!" Squishy shouted at the group, pointing in the direction they had come from. "At least two dozen!"

Aiden picked up his shield, sword, and ran to Squishy's side. Grape joined them, daggers ready for the oncoming fight. Brittany came running up behind them, bow ready and aimed at the soldiers.

"We don't have to be quiet anymore, right?" Rina asked Teddy as the two stood at the back of the group.

"No, child." Teddy replied.

Brittany let loose arrow after arrow, each striking their opponents, either in a weak point or in their helmets, distracting them as they charged. Aiden and Squishy met the group head on, Squishy swinging his hammer with the speed of which the soldiers wielded their swords, crushing anyone it met. Aiden dodged, parried, blocked all attacks that were sent his way and countered with his own, however, his were far more powerful than that of the soldiers.

A swing of his sword landed flat into the side of a guard, devastating his armor and sending the man flying into the others. Grape maneuvered her way to pick off anyone who dodged Aiden or Squishy, taking advantage of their lack of awareness on the battlefield. Teddy had done as he had before, summoning roots to entangle the soldier's feet, making them easy targets for the rest of his group.

Rina hesitated, wanting to try a spell that she feared, but felt that it was needed. "Lightening." She muttered under her breath. Hearing what she had said, Teddy looked down at her in shock, unsure what she was planning. Rina counted fourteen archers that threatened her family.

She focused on them, counting each one in her head, as she uttered the word, thunder shook the heavens as fourteen lightning bolts came from the clouds to strike each guard, killing all of them instantaneously. The group turned to look at Teddy, who was staring at Rina, amazed at the power of the spell. Aiden was the only one who looked directly to Rina, stunned that she had been able to control such force.

Shaking his head, Teddy said. "Let's go! There will be more."

Brittany followed the group, staring at her children, astonished at how much they had changed since she had been gone. Aiden fought with such skill and strength that she had never seen within him, reminding her of their father, feeling pride as she witnessed the change, and Rina, she had an aura about her, something magical in nature, that Brittany couldn't place, she radiated with power.

"Over here..." Brittany heard a guard yell, from above them, only to fall over with an arrow sticking out of his neck. As she looked up in the direction the arrow would have come from, she saw another creature she would not have expected to be with her children. (Of course, they would have more allies to make this mission successful.) She thought to herself.

Squishy signaled for Arlington to be ready to leave as the group entered the bottom of the tower. Teddy told everyone to stand back as he closed his eyes and muttered incomprehensibly. A second later, more roots sprouted from the ground, dividing the wall of the tower, creating a frame of a door. Once the frame was complete, Teddy opened his eyes and walked towards the wall, placing one paw against the stone within the frame, a red aura emanating from his hand as the stone crumbled into dust. "Let's go!"

Epilogue

"Quick! Over here!" Jr. shouted to the group as they ran from the tower.

The group swiftly ran in his direction, into a blacksmith's shop that was closed for the night, leaving it empty inside.

"What are you doing here?" Brittany asked Aiden and Rina who were now attached to her, hugging her tightly as Ellie ran around her in circles.

"Jr., Arlington, keep an eye out and let us know when it's safe to leave here." Teddy told the two hunters.

"We had to save you mommy!" Rina said, her eyes filled with tears. "We missed you so much!"

"But how?" Brittany asked, hugging her children tightly, kissing them on their heads and checking to make sure that they were not harmed.

"I sent them to help." Teddy answered, pointing at Squishy, Grape, Arlington, and Jr. "As soon as I sensed the magic, I sent them to help whoever it was. They were too late to help you and your husband though. I'm sorry."

"We found them in the woods and helped them." Squishy added.

"Who are you?" Brittany asked, eyeing the old Bermion.

"I am Teddy, a Master Wizard." Teddy replied.

"Wait... You said you sensed magic?" Brittany realized, turning to face her children. "So, they weren't lying when they asked about it... Which one of you two?"

"Me..." Rina said, stifling her tears. "I'm sorry mommy!"

"Oh sweetie!" Brittany replied. "There's no reason to be sorry. I just wished I knew so I could have protected you two."

"We're okay mom." Aiden added.

"I see that." She commented. "My strong little man is growing up so fast!"

"Mom!" Aiden replied, embarrassed.

"What about your father?" Brittany asked.

"We don't know where he is." Grape answered. "We think Cladon has him up north."

"Now's our chance!" Jr. Told the group.

"Will you join us?" Teddy asked Brittany.

"For now. Once we're safe, we have a lot to talk about." Brittany replied, still unsure if she should trust the group.

After a few minutes of rest, the group left the blacksmith shop, making their way through the city as the sun rose in the distance. The cobblestone streets were empty since the soldiers were now ahead of them, thinking that they kept fleeing after they broke out of the prison.

The higher the sun rose, the more visible the group became, losing the shadows that they used for cover. They headed south, a direction that no one would think they would go, for only the desert waited for them below the city. Teddy explained that if they wanted the best chance to escape from Cladon's gaze, the desert would be the best choice.

As they ran, they came across only a few soldiers here and there, easily dispatched by arrows from Jr., Arlington, and Brittany. Having a third archer made their journey a lot quieter than before. As the sun rose higher, the citizens started leaving their homes, giving the group another obstacle to get past. Teddy quickly used a spell to make anyone they came across, fall asleep where they stood.

"There's the outer wall." Squishy stated to the group. "Be alert, we're likely to run into soldiers near here."

As if on cue, five dozen soldiers came from the west, patrolling the perimeter. The group quickly hid behind a building, concealing them from being noticed.

"Listen up!" The leader of the soldiers shouted. "We have orders to take the old Bermion and the children alive! All others, use force!"

"Yes Sir!" The soldiers replied.

"They're still within the city walls, the east and west exits are covered." The Captain continued. "North is unlikely! That leaves the south! We will defend this and capture them if they come this way!"

"What should we do?" Arlington asked.

"Can you three spread-out, and shoot from the rooftops?" Aiden asked, pointing to Jr., Arlington, and his mother. "If we can distract them from multiple directions, it will make it easier for Grape, Squishy, Ellie, and I to go in and attack up close."

Brittany stared at Aiden, surprised at the tactical prowess he had. "That sounds good to me, son."

Nodding to his mother, Aiden continued. "Teddy, Rina, can you two focus your magic on their center? Dividing them in two directions and forcing them closer to the arrows."

"Yes." Teddy and Rina agreed.

"I'm so very proud of you two." Brittany said before she ran off to her perch on the rooftops, causing Aiden to blush a little.

Jr., Brittany, and Arlington were ready on top of their own roofs, spread-out enough to confuse the enemy in their direction, awaiting the signal to fire. Teddy and Rina concentrated on the center of the formation, both agreeing that an explosive spell would cause the most chaos. Nodding to each other, the two released their magic, triggering a fire to erupt at the center of the soldier's formation.

The soldiers closest to the blast, died instantly. The explosion caused the group to disperse as planned, forcing them in the direction of the archers, who released a volley of arrows on the unsuspecting victims. With the soldiers split in two, Aiden and Squishy led the charge on both sides.

Squishy taking the right, Aiden taking the left. One by one, the soldiers fell, the chaos distracting them from their training. Rina and Teddy followed the group on their assault, aiding their fights whenever one of the hand to hand combatants were getting overwhelmed. Three soldiers tried to overpower Aiden, only to be met with a fire in their faces from the two wizards, blinding them and making them easy targets for him to take out.

Any of the soldier's, on the outside of the formation, that had turned to fight, were met with arrows in the back. Aiden's plan was flawless and required minimum effort on the group. In a matter of minutes, the cluster of over fifty soldiers was down to a handful that were trying to flee and were easily picked off by the archers on the roof.

"There's more coming!" Brittany yelled, pointing in the direction of the prison just before releasing arrows on the newcomers.

"Keep them occupied for a moment!" Teddy told the group as he ran towards the wall that separated them from the desert.

Arlington and Jr. joined the group, fighting the army of soldiers with their paws, long since running out of arrows. Even though the bulk of the soldier presence went north for the war, there were hundreds of soldiers still in the city. Rina used her magic, less effective than she had done previously, running low on energy.

Where she had done mass explosive spells to take out many enemies, now she used smaller, more focused spells to help keep the soldiers from overtaking her friends and family. A well-timed fireball on a soldier that tried to flank Aiden, or a single root that sprung from the ground to entangle the feet of another who attempted to overwhelm Grape. Rina didn't think, she just reacted to each situation, she had to keep them safe and would do everything in her power to do so.

The Bermion and Kaiine used their size and strength to overpower most of the soldiers, tossing them into their comrades, giving them a little more space. Aiden fought side by side with them, a bloodlust that they had never seen before in a human. He didn't fight to kill, he fought to protect, a far better motivator. Aiden swept through the waves of soldiers as if possessed by a God, taking out one after another, never losing a step.

Soldiers began climbing onto the roof where Brittany stayed, firing what little arrows she had left. The first soldier to reach her, swung his sword recklessly, only to be parried by her bow, and followed by a kick that sent him tumbling back off the roof into his friends. Brittany picked up the sword the soldier dropped.

Two more soldiers made it to her perch, each willing to take her life if given the opportunity. The first soldier was far too slow to hit her, she easily dodged his attack, thrusting her sword into his chest in response. The second one was now upon her, ducking, she managed to dodge another attack that would have taken off her head.

Seeing that her mother was getting surrounded, Rina cast a fireball that hit the soldier on the roof, knocking him off the edge. Rina watched as her mother took the chance to leave her post to join the others fighting below. She looked over the battle, looking for any one that posed an immediate threat to her family, for all of them were becoming family to her.

"No..." She whispered as she saw dozens of archers come from down the street. She looked at Aiden, who was fighting four soldiers on his own, having the upper hand against all of them. Squishy and Jr. fought side by side, Jr. covering for Squishy after he swung his hammer, which would leave him open, but Jr. would follow up, protecting his weak points.

Grape, Arlington, and Ellie fought together as well, the three fought as one, tearing through the ranks of the Kaskian soldiers. One would attack, then the other, then Ellie would come from behind and take out another, all fighting to protect each other, holding their ground.

The archers were getting closer and Rina was running low on energy, she could feel it draining from her, but she had to do something. She was the only one who saw them. Then it hit her, she remembered her necklace resting around her neck, a necklace that was filled with power.

"Please work..." She muttered to herself. Rina pulled the trinket from around her neck, focusing on pulling energy from it, energy that lay deep inside, closing her eyes, Rina focused harder, concentrating on the battle and the archers who were almost in range, they were the target, all of them had to go. "Lightening!" She shouted with such force that thunder shook the battlefield, causing a quake that knocked everyone off balance as lightning spewed from the sky, one after another, bolts of lightning struck down not only the archers, but all the remaining soldiers, ending the battle with the single spell.

Brittany rushed to Rina's side as she fell to the ground, energy spent, Rina blacked out after the spell. "What's wrong with her?!" Brittany yelled.

"She used too much energy." Aiden replied, rushing to her side. "She'll be okay, she just needs time to recover."

"Almost done!" Teddy stated while focusing on the wall, a wall that was too thick to use brute force to break. The south wall was not created to keep just the sand out, it was created to stand against anything that would come from the desert, Cladon had reinforced it with magic to keep it strong under any assault.

Teddy had to focus on finding the wards intertwined in the stone before he could break it. "Found it..." He muttered, sensing the spell that held the stone together. Focusing on the spell, Teddy reached out with his mind, grabbing the thread, and pulled it from the wall, dispersing the magic into the air. Once the magic had departed the wall, Teddy placed his paw against the hard stone, uttered the word

"Break" which caused that part of the wall to crumble into a million pieces, showing the desert that waited for them on the other side.

Brittany picked up Rina in her arms and ran with the group through the opening of the walls as they saw more soldiers coming for them in all directions. Too many soldiers for them to fight. Brittany and Rina were the first to make it through the gap in the wall where Teddy waited on the other side, telling her to keep going and get a safe distance away from the wall.

Aiden followed his mother and sister, running a few yards into the dry harsh desert, the sun high in the sky, bearing down all its weight on them. They watched as the rest of their group followed them, one by one, they all made it through and caught up with them. Aiden watched as the soldiers started to pour through the break in the wall too. Horrified at the numbers that followed them.

Teddy was the last to join them, standing between the group and the soldiers who stayed near the wall, waiting for their numbers to make it through to overwhelm them. Teddy raised his staff high in the sky, the gem glowed brighter than that of the sun, a golden aura emanating from Teddy, an aura that drew the sand from the desert into it.

Teddy's aura was mixing with the sand, becoming one. Aiden flinched as a breeze picked up, slowly becoming more aggressive, until finally blowing so hard it nearly knocked the group over. He raised his hand to block the sand from berating his face as he watched, stunned, when he realized exactly what Teddy was doing.

The faster the wind moved, the more sand it picked up until it was a full-blown sandstorm. The group watched as the sandstorm overtook Teddy, blocking him from their sight as it also separated the soldiers from them. They waited for what felt like an eternity until they finally saw the old Bermion emerge from the sandstorm, staff raised high, with a blue aura protecting him from the hostile force he created.

"The war has begun."